PATRICIA ROBINS

THE RUNAWAYS

Complete and Unabridged

LINFORD
Leicester

First published in Great Britain in 1962 by
Hurst & Blackett Limited
An imprint of
The Hutchinson Group
London

First Linford Edition
published 2013
by arrangement with
The Hutchinson Group
London

A catalogue record for this book is available
from the British Library.

ISBN 978–1–4448–1722–5

Published by
F. A. Thorpe (Publishing)
Anstey, Leicestershire

Set by Words & Graphics Ltd.
Anstey, Leicestershire
Printed and bound in Great Britain by
T. J. International Ltd., Padstow, Cornwall

This book is printed on acid-free paper

1

'How much further, Rocky?'

Judith looked anxiously at the slim figure behind the steering wheel. It seemed as if they had been driving for days rather than hours, and everything had conspired to make the journey as difficult as possible.

Rocky suddenly slammed on the brakes and the car skidded slightly on the dark, wet road. He swore under his breath and then, without looking at Judith, he opened the car door and disappeared, bareheaded, into the driving rain. For a moment his tall, slim figure was silhouetted in the light of the headlamps; then she saw the faint glimmer of his torch against the white sign-post. A minute or two later he climbed back into the car, a gust of rain blowing in with him.

In those brief moments his tweed

jacket had become soaked and the rain was dripping down his white face in rivulets. His voice was flat and emotionless as he said:

'We must have missed the road just after Carlisle. That signpost said half-a-mile to Rockcliffe, wherever that might be.'

He sounded cross — almost as if it were her fault they had lost their way. Perhaps it *was* her fault, Judith thought miserably. She had been the navigator, tracing out their route from Yeovil to Gretna Green along the thin red lines of the A.A. book. But it was Rocky who had said at Carlisle:

'You can put that thing away now. We're nearly there.'

Tactfully she decided this was not the moment to argue and she reached for the A.A. book and studied the map once more.

'I'm afraid we went wrong at Stanwix,' she said at length. 'It must have been when we were behind that big furniture lorry, darling. But it's not going to matter too much. After we've passed through Rockcliffe we can get back on the A74 and then it's only a couple of miles to Gretna.'

Still he did not smile or put out a hand consolingly to hers. She bit her lip, trying not to let the deep depression that had been gathering inside her gain control. Rocky must be tired. He'd driven the first six hours non-stop on top of a hard day's work. Their only halt at the transport café for a meal had been as brief as possible and then he had been back behind the wheel once more, fighting all the way through ceaseless driving rain that limited visibility to a few yards, sometimes to inches. The monotonous click-click, click-click of the windscreen wipers had played on her nerves. How much more aggravating must it have been to Rocky, who could never take his eyes from the dark road ahead.

Judith wished she had accepted her father's offer of a course of driving lessons on her seventeenth birthday last summer. She had always wanted to learn to drive, and her father had been more than a little surprised when she refused. She hadn't felt able to give him the true reason — that she wanted every spare moment free to be with Rocky; that even those few hours a week were hours far too precious to miss. Until now, she hadn't regretted her decision. No one in their right senses would prefer to sit beside a driving instructor, learning how to cope with gears, when the alternative meant lying on the river bank on a hot summer's evening with Rocky's arms about her, or dancing on a Saturday evening, or playing tennis together at the Club.

How fortunate for both of them that they were so fond of tennis, for they could meet at the Club without her parents realizing that this was just another date with Rocky, of whom they seemed so stupidly to disapprove. Neither her father nor her mother had actually refused to allow her to go out with Rocky, but they said quite firmly that twice a week was enough; that it was quite wrong at her age to limit herself to one boy-friend, and that she must never be out later than midnight and then only when they knew who she was with and where she was going.

Judith had tried so hard not to feel that they were being old-fashioned and unreasonable. All parents refused to recognize that their children had grown up, she told herself. They still thought of her as a child rather than a woman. How could they know that love had transformed her in one moment from child to adult!

Judith had never been particularly close to either parent, perhaps because she had been born very late in their lives and the gulf of forty years was too great to be bridged. She'd never really noticed it until she met Rocky and then she was suddenly aware that she could never explain to these quiet, elderly, grey-haired people that nothing in the world mattered to her except Rocky.

She didn't expect them to understand. How could they? Their love for each other was a quiet, friendly affection that belonged to a generation who had been brought up to think of sex as a necessary evil. She and Rocky had often discussed it and thought with sympathy how incomplete that generation's youth must have been.

They were supremely glad that they belonged to the youth of today who could accept that sex was part of love and marriage, and something to be gloried in rather than to be ashamed of. Of course, she and Rocky did differ on one point. Rocky believed that trial marriages, as he called them, were good. He'd wanted to make love to her, fully and completely, not for his sake only but for hers, too. He wanted them both to be quite sure that they were physically suited, as they were in every other way.

Judith, much as she yearned to belong to Rocky in the way that he wanted so much, still could not bring herself to accept the necessity for experience of this sort before marriage. Her love for Rocky was so complete, such a deep certainty in her mind and heart and thoughts, that she never doubted the complete success of the physical side of their relationship.

In some strange way she could not quite understand, Rocky's physical need for her seemed greater than hers for him! Inevitably every evening ended in long, passionate embraces and Rocky's voice, urgent and desperate, begging her to give way. She had read enough to know that this continual tension must be bad for him, and she herself had felt her resolve to wait for marriage grow weaker as the summer days passed to autumn and autumn to winter. Now they could no longer lie on the river bank and watch the stars come out. The desperate search for somewhere to be alone together was becoming increasingly hopeless. Rocky was not welcome in her parents' home and although her mother and father were polite enough to Rocky when she asked him back for a meal, or to hear a new record, they would no more have left her alone with him in the drawing-room than they would countenance a request to share her summer holiday with him. She knew they didn't trust him but put this down to their out-of-date ideas on modern behaviour and felt slightly hurt by the fact that they did not, at least, trust her.

With Rocky's parents the situation was not much better. He was studying for his City and Guilds examination whilst serving his student-apprenticeship with an aircraft company. His father was in the same firm and was tremendously ambitious for his only son. So far, Rocky had done very well and his father bitterly resented that Judith should have come into his life to cause rival interest to his career. Rocky denied she was any such thing. He told his parents a thousand times that Judith gave him an incentive to work harder and to get on; that since Judith had to be home at a reasonably early hour, he could do his studies after his dates with her. He often worked until two or three in the morning and even Judith had had to admit that his mother was right when she said he was beginning to look pale and exhausted. Mrs. Rockingham made little effort to conceal the fact that she considered Judith to blame.

These were the factors that had brought them to the momentous decision to get married. It seemed to both of them the answer to all their problems. Married, they would, as Rocky so much desired, belong to each other completely. Since they would be able to share the long hours of the night together, they would have no need to waste the evening dancing, walking, playing tennis; Rocky could come home and work at his studies while she took care of him and the house. There would be no time for housework during the day since she, too, must keep on her job as secretarial assistant to the local vet. They had worked out a budget for themselves and with their two pay-packets they could afford to live, if not in their own home, at least in furnished rooms. In five years, if they were careful, they could save enough to pay the deposit on a house.

For three weeks they had spent most of their moments together planning how they would live when they were married. It was only in the last week that both had suddenly realized that neither his parents nor hers would give consent. It was Judith who had swept aside this particular hurdle by suggesting Gretna Green. Rocky had been uncertain. For one thing, it would be extremely difficult to get three weeks away from work when he had not long ago had a fortnight off for his summer holiday. For another, if either set of parents reported them to the police, it could get into the daily papers and he wasn't sure that his firm would keep him on since he, being the elder, would be held responsible. Yet, at the same time, it was Rocky who couldn't stand the thought of four more years to wait!

Thinking back, as she sat silently at Rocky's side in his mother's ancient Morris, bumping along the bad, Scottish by-road only a mile from their destination, Judith recalled that the ultimate decision to come had been Rocky's. His uncertainty had affected her in the end and two nights ago she had told him she had made up her mind to drop the whole idea.

Some inner mature wisdom told her that the outcome could not be happy unless Rocky were absolutely certain this runaway marriage was the right thing for them both. Had she but known it, this decision was the one weapon that could make him swing to the opposite point of view. From that moment, he would hear nothing against their elopement. He swept aside her questions about a job during the three weeks residence in Scotland before they could obtain a licence, their lack of a car — he would borrow his mother's — where and how they would live. He seemed suddenly to be fired with a god-like enthusiasm that could overcome any problem and cope with any emergency, and when Judith had slipped out of her house after tea, with her suitcase, she, too, had been borne along on a wave of exhilaration and determination to brave anything for each other.

When had this wave receded like the outgoing tide, leaving her mind and heart like the wet sand, deserted, lonely and afraid? On that long, bleak stretch of road between Shap Fell and Penrith, where the fan-belt broke and she had had to spend a lonely half-hour in the car while Rocky went in a passing lorry to the next garage for a replacement? Or was it before that, when somewhere around Shrewsbury the overworked windscreen wipers had packed in altogether and they had to stop every hundred yards or so, taking it in turns to get out and wipe the windscreen until they found an all-night garage with the right size of blades in stock?

Surely they had laughed about it at the time, or had there been something forced about Rocky's smile? When had she begun to feel that Fate was against them and not with them on their flight to happiness?

'There's the main road ahead!'

Rocky's voice sounded more cheerful, and immediately Judith's spirits rose. So long as he was happy she didn't mind what happened. She didn't mind the bumping or the cold or even the driving rain outside, providing Rocky went on loving her and wanting her and not regretting their decision to run away. For his sake, she was more than willing to face the inevitable scene that must follow with her parents and his when they went home again. It wouldn't matter. Nothing would matter then, because she would be Rocky's wife.

As if sensing her mood, Rocky took one hand from the steering-wheel and felt for hers in the darkness, finding it and giving it a squeeze.

'Hope we'll find somewhere open, darling. Must be about four o'clock. Have you thought what we're going to say when we do get there? Is it to be Mr. and Mrs. or do we register separately?'

She looked at him quickly, anxiously, and then turned away again uneasily. How stupid of her not to have thought about this. Would Rocky think she was terribly naive or priggish to want to hold on a little longer, now that she knew for sure there were only twenty-one days before they could be married? The waiting would not be hard for her, but Rocky might think it silly since there was no doubt now that they would be married so soon. Ought she to go through with it? Strange that she should be thinking of such a night as an ordeal to be 'gone through'! It wasn't quite that. It was the thought that they would have to sign false names in the register, that people might guess they were eloping since they were obviously English, under age, and unlikely to be arriving at a place like Gretna Green at four o'clock in the morning, in mid-December, on an annual holiday.

She tried to explain to Rocky how difficult it would be to convince anyone they were in fact a married couple.

'I couldn't care less!' Rocky replied. 'After all, we are going to be married very soon. Please, Judith!'

She felt suddenly a hundred years older than Rocky. He sounded so like a small boy asking for a sweet. He didn't seem to realize that they would be defeating the whole object of their coming here if she gave way now. She wanted their first night together to be perfect, free of fear, of criticism by the outside world, with nothing and no one to break into the magic circle of their love. She felt quite sure that were he less tired and able to think more clearly, Rocky would agree with her.

Quite suddenly the large road-sign flashed into the headlights — GRETNA GREEN — and Judith was saved an immediate reply.

Rocky was staring out of the side-windows, his eyes searching for a hotel. There was no sign of a light anywhere. He turned the car at the far end of the village and crawled back again in low gear, then pulled the car up on the side of the road with a muttered exclamation.

'Not a damn thing open anywhere! Gosh, Judy, I am an idiot. I should have booked in somewhere days ago. Now what are we going to do?'

'We could sleep here in the car for an hour or two, then perhaps we can get some breakfast and ask about rooms. We don't really want to stay in a hotel, do we? If anyone . . . ' she paused, uneasily. ' . . . What I mean is, if anyone should guess where we've gone, the hotels would be the first place for them to look for us.'

Rocky drew in his breath sharply.

'You make us sound like criminals,' he said roughly.

Judith tried to smile.

'Well, I suppose we are fugitives from

the conventions if not from the law. It seems silly when we aren't doing anything wrong. We aren't, are we Rocky?'

Rocky turned away from her and stared out of the window. A car flashed by with an angry roar, and scattered a shower of muddy water in front of his face with impersonal insult.

'Oh, God!' he said, wearily. 'I'm damned if I know. I wish it weren't so blasted cold.'

Stupidly, he'd rushed out of the house when he got back from work, remembering his suit-case but forgetting his overcoat. It hadn't been too cold then at five o'clock but it was at least ten degrees colder this side of the Border, and hellishly damp. Moreover, his tweed jacket was soaking and he would have given his eyes for a steaming hot bath. He thought of his comfortable divan bed at home, and then immediately felt guilty. Poor little Judy! She must be just as cold and depressed as he was, and, bless her, she

17

hadn't grumbled once.

He turned and ran his hands gently over the smooth, golden crown of her head. Her hair was the very first thing he had noticed about her that night last spring at the Tennis Club Dance. She'd been standing with her back towards him and he said to himself, half-seriously:

'If she looks as good from the front as she does from the back, that's my idea of a smashing blonde.'

The fact that Judith wore her hair in an out-of-date, smooth, page-boy bob had made her stand out from the rest of the crowd of girls, with their bouffant piled-up curls. Intrigued, he'd edged around till he could see her full-face, and at that moment she had looked up and caught him staring at her, and he felt his heart miss a beat as those incredibly large gentian-blue eyes had smiled shyly into his own.

Regardless of the fact that there were two men standing talking to her, he'd pushed his way past the people standing between them and had asked her for the next dance. Equally surprisingly, she had accepted without a word to her companions.

At first he hadn't thought much beyond the fact that she attracted him physically as no other girl had ever done. Each time he saw her he knew there had to be another time, and another, until seeing her and being with her had become a kind of obsession which clouded his waking thoughts and disturbed his dreams. It was only when his younger sister had remarked in her teasing way that he was obviously madly in love with Judith Bryant, that he realized this must be true. He'd had other girl friends but there had been nothing more than a casual flirtation. He'd never felt casual about Judy. Once or twice he had almost wished he'd never met her. He knew that he ought to be concentrating on his exam. He was tremendously ambitious and was as determined as his father to become someone of importance. But somehow

Judy came between him and his erstwhile enthusiasm for his career. But he was able to argue with himself that Judith was a good influence, since she gave him another reason for making good.

She nestled against him now, responsive to the touch of his hand on her head, leaning against his shoulder with complete trust and confidence in him. If only he had as much confidence in himself! However much he might say that their elopement was as much her decision as his, he nevertheless felt that being the elder by three years, the ultimate responsibility must be with him.

He gave a worried frown as he tried not to ask himself whether they were doing the right thing. For the moment, cold, tired, considerably exhausted by the long journey, his desire to possess her was dormant. There was no longer that urgent need of her to overrule the cold logic of thought. Unbidden and unwelcome came a hundred doubts about the future. He'd only got £50 in the bank, and how long was this going to last, especially if he lost his job! Supposing Judith's father came rushing up to Gretna to drag her back, the way he'd so often read of other fathers, in the daily papers? He'd never imagined, reading those stories, that one day he might be in the same position as the fellow he'd thought of as a silly fool. His face flushed in the darkness as he imagined the comments his fellow-apprentices might make, and then tried quickly to put such thoughts from him, as if in some way they were disloyal to Judith.

If only they had both been older. The old envied the young, but he'd never been able to understand why. Older men had all the advantages, a secure place in the world, money in the bank, and freedom to do as they pleased. If it were five years hence, he and Judith could have defied their parents and been married without all these complications and, he was forced to face the fact, risks.

He wanted desperately to sleep, as Judith now slept, calmly and peacefully in his arms; but tired as he was, the thoughts kept crowding through his mind; what kind of job could he possibly find in a place like Gretna Green? There would be no potato-picking or agricultural work at this time of the year, and little passing traffic to necessitate an extra garage hand. Perhaps he'd be able to get something in Carlisle. Just as well he'd brought the car . . .

The thought of his mother's car brought a fresh wave of unease. In a way, Mrs. Rockingham had always spoilt him, letting him have everything within her power to give. Any time in the past, when he wanted to borrow the Morris, she'd been only too happy for him to have it. But there was no good pretending that she'd taken to Judith, and once she realized just why he had borrowed the car without asking, she might object very strongly. Not that she could do very much about it, since he had left no address where he had gone. His note had merely indicated that he was going away for a few weeks but she was not to worry, that he was not in any trouble, and would get in touch with her on his return.

Now this note struck him as being the height of stupidity. Of course she would worry. He'd never disappeared from home for three weeks before without everyone knowing just where he was going, and for how long, and it stood to reason that Judith's parents when they found her missing would put two and two together and get in touch with his father. They'd know that there was only one place they could be, and then a word to the police and there'd be no difficulty at all in tracing them through the registration number of the Morris.

What a mess it all was! He'd have to get rid of the car somehow. Perhaps he could get a local garage to take it in on the pretext that it needed a thorough overhaul. Maybe there'd be a bus into Carlisle or perhaps he could hitch a lift on passing lorries. To hide the car had now become a matter of urgency, he realized. It was possible that Judith's father had already notified the police. With only a moment's hesitation at the sight of Judith's white, exhausted face, he shook her gently into wakefulness.

'We've got to get a move on,' he told her, abruptly. 'It's nearly five o'clock. There ought to be somebody about, somewhere.'

He started the engine.

'Look, there's a light,' Judith said, eagerly. For the moment the future had no meaning. She was too tired to care about tomorrow. All she wanted was a hot bath, a cup of tea, and bed. Rocky breathed a sigh of relief and drove towards the light. Rather like the end of the rainbow, it seemed to recede from them as they turned down narrow roads and then into a bumpy lane in an effort to reach it. At last they could see the shadowy outline of a small stone farmhouse, and Rocky stopped the car with a jolt in what he realized must be the farmyard.

Leaving Judith in the car, he climbed out and walked stiffly to the door.

There was no bell, but a heavy iron horseshoe which he rapped urgently against the wooden door. The cold east wind which seemed to have followed the rain beat against his still-damp clothes, and by the time the door was inched open he was shivering violently. A round-faced, rosy-cheeked woman in a long tweed skirt, covered by a fresh white apron, stared out at him suspiciously, an old-fashioned oil-lamp held aloft. Rocky stepped forward quickly.

'Excuse me, but is there a chance that you have a spare room?' he asked. 'We've been driving all night and can't find a hotel open.'

The woman held the lamp closer to his face, peering at him as if to judge the authenticity of his story. He was suddenly conscious of the dishevelled state of his clothes, and in the same instant aware that he had asked for one room only. There had been no thought in his mind of Judith. It had been an instinctive remark, since a small farm-house such as this would have been unlikely to have a number of spare rooms to offer passing guests.

As if reading his thoughts, she said in a strong Scottish accent:

'Is the room you'll be wanting for you and your guid wife?'

He nodded, unwilling to speak the lie.

'Will you wait there a wee while, while I speak to my man?' she told him, curtly, and disappeared back inside the house, closing the door on him firmly.

'Isn't it any good?' Judith called to him from the window of the car.

He went across to her and said, bleakly:

'She's gone to ask her husband if it's all right. I had to tell her you were my wife. I think they've only got one spare room.'

He sensed, rather than saw, the swift rush of colour into her cheeks, but she didn't say anything.

'Don't worry about it, Judith. I'm not going to make you do anything you don't want to do. For the time being,

26

the most important thing is to find somewhere where we can both sleep — '

He broke off as the door opened and
the farmer's wife beckoned to them to
come in.

Rocky grabbed the two suitcases
from the back seat of the car and he
and Judith stepped forward into the
lighted kitchen.

'The kettle's nearly on the boil,'
she said bustling them both forward
towards the range. Judith walked into
the wave of warmth, thankfully. She was
so stiff with cold that normal thought
had given way to numb acceptance. But
Rocky was relieved to see she had kept
on her gloves as she held her hands
towards the range for warmth, lest this
kindly woman might realize she was
not, after all, Rocky's wife.

'Will I be showing you the room, the
noo?' the woman was asking Rocky.
Rocky looked at Judith questioningly,
and with an effort she moved away
from the range and followed them up
the narrow, wooden stair-case. The

carpet was thread-bare, but spotlessly clean, and the large bedroom with its huge double oak bedstead, though sparsely furnished, was polished and shining in its simplicity.

'It's all I can offer you,' the farmer's wife was saying. 'The bed's no aired so I'll be putting a stone bottle in it a wee while. There'll be water, too, for washing if ye want it. Will ye come down for your breakfast?'

'I couldn't eat a thing, Rocky,' Judith said. 'If I could just have a cup of tea? Maybe you could bring it up to me. I think I'll go straight to bed.'

Rocky nodded his head. He wondered if she wanted to be alone or if she really wasn't hungry. There didn't seem much point worrying about it. He could do with a meal; in fact, he'd only just realized how frightfully hungry he was.

Left alone at last, Judith unpacked her suitcase in the flickering light of the candle. She realized that there was no hope of a bath but the feathered quilt on the bed promised warmth. She pulled out the thin, diaphanous nightdress that had lain this last six months in her bottom-drawer, part of the trousseau she had started to collect, and which she had never expected to need so soon. There hadn't been room in the one small suitcase for all her things, and because she'd wanted so much to look beautiful for Rocky on her wedding night, she had packed only this one flimsy garment for the night. She looked down at it with misgivings. It would hardly serve to keep her warm but the matching négligé would at least help to cover her nakedness.

As she hurriedly pulled off her tweed suit, she wondered why, having chosen this attire especially for Rocky's delight, she should now feel so frightened at the thought of wearing it. Outside in the car just now, Rocky had promised he wasn't going to try to make love to her unless she wanted him to do so. She could trust him. It was stupid to feel like a frightened school-girl.

All the same, she completed her undressing as quickly as possible and jumped in between the cold sheets, listening all the time for the sound of Rocky's footsteps on the stairs. Through the thin floor-boards, she could hear the noises from the kitchen below and once or twice a deep voice that she supposed belonged to the farmer. She was so cold, in spite of the warm covers, that even the wish for a cup of tea had left her, and she seemed unable to stop the shivering in every part of her body. But gradually, as the minutes ticked past, the warmth came back and she was almost asleep when there was a brief knock on the door and the rattle of a tea-cup against a saucer.

She knew it was Rocky. But for the first time since she'd known him, she didn't want to see him. She closed her eyes tightly and tried to steady her breathing as the door opened and he came towards her. She heard him put the cup and saucer down beside her; presently his footsteps drew away from her and the door closed quietly behind him. Then she felt ashamed of her pretence. It would have cost her nothing to thank him for the tea, to hold his hand for a moment, to kiss him — if that was what he wanted. Perhaps, she thought, deceit is like a snowball; once you start pretending you have to go on. If only she could hibernate for three weeks, and wake up to find herself truly married to Rocky . . . A moment later she was asleep.

2

It was not yet half-past six, but neither Mr. Bryant nor his wife had been able to stay in bed a moment longer.

'We've just got to do *something*,' Olive Bryant said to her husband across the table in the breakfast-room. 'After all, Harold, Judith's only seventeen.'

Harold Bryant looked at his wife with irritation. As if he didn't know how old his daughter was!

'This tea's cold,' he said, pushing the pot towards her.

He noticed her face then, drawn and tired from her sleepless night, and felt sorry for his bad temper. It wasn't fair to take his own anxiety out on her, poor dear. If only she'd had the good sense to look in Judith's bottom-drawer last night. The idea had first occurred to her at five o'clock this morning and only then had they both realized that Judith had not merely run away from home, but that she had in all probability run away to join young Rockingham.

For the hundredth time he took up Judith's note and scrutinized it as if hoping for some further lead.

Dear Daddy,

How childish her handwriting was. Absurd to think of Judith as a woman old enough to get married. She was only a girl, not a year out of school.

I'm going away for three weeks. I wish I could tell you why, but I can't. Please believe me that I know what I'm doing and that there is absolutely no need for you or Mother to be worried about me. When I come back, I will explain everything. I have plenty of money with me and I shall be quite all right. Your loving, Judith.

'Plenty of money!' She couldn't possibly have much. She had an account at his Bank and naturally, as Manager, he knew quite well that she had never had more than thirty or forty pounds in it. He gave her quite a

33

generous clothes allowance but she hadn't been saving this. He knew that she'd been buying clothes for her 'bottom-drawer', which his wife had only just informed him existed. So Judith must have been thinking for some time about getting married. If only it were a bit later in the day, the Bank would be open and he could go and have a look at her account, discover whether she'd drawn the rest of her savings in the last day or two.

'I think we ought to get in touch with the police,' his wife said for the third time. He tried not to let his impatience with her be too apparent.

'Do sit down, my dear, and stop making ridiculous suggestions,' he said quietly but forcefully. 'You know very well that in my position we can't have any scandal. It's perfectly obvious now — at least to me — that Judith's gone off with young Rockingham. All we've got to do is to find her and bring her back. And you, my dear, could start praying that it's not too late.'

Olive Bryant was a frail, timid-looking woman who had never really had to fend for herself. When she was young, she'd been a little like Judith to look at, with fair golden hair and enormous blue eyes. But while Judith had inherited her mother's erstwhile beauty, she had also acquired her father's strong, determined nature. It was this strength of character that had helped Harold Bryant to rise from being the son of a small-town butcher to the responsible, enviable position as Manager of the Amalgamated Bank. He was a County Councillor and a Rotarian, and in general a respected citizen of the country town in which they lived.

This status was one Harold Bryant regarded jealously. He'd married Olive Bryant for two reasons; partly because her fair, pale beauty attracted him, but also because she was the daughter of the local vicar who had come from a very good family. He had never doubted his own ability to get on and he wanted the kind of wife who would be able to take her place at his side when he got there.

As Judith had instinctively guessed, it was not a marriage of love in its true sense, but they had got along very well together for the past thirty years. And although he was the dominant partner in no uncertain terms, he was fond of his wife and kind to her, and he'd never once looked at another woman since the day she walked down the aisle on his arm.

He'd been too ambitious to want a family at first, and by the time he was forty it seemed as if fate didn't intend to bless them with a family, in any event. Then Judith had arrived, and like a lot of men he welcomed this pretty little daughter as an unexpected delight for his old age. It soon became apparent to him that Judith was much more intelligent than her mother, and whilst it was not part of his nature to spoil her, his love for her was genuine and unselfish. He had never consciously denied her anything he had felt to be for her good, She'd had an excellent education at a small private day-school and he hadn't stood in her way when she wanted a secretarial training rather than the finishing school he'd had in mind. Secretly, he'd hoped that she would think of starting work in his bank and it had been somewhat of a disappointment when she announced that she wanted to take a job with Gavin Pelham, their local vet. Of course, Judith had always been mad about animals, and because of her mother's asthma she'd not been able to have a puppy or a kitten like other children she knew. So he'd agreed, and as far as he knew she had settled down well and liked her job, and Pelham seemed very pleased with her. In fact, they'd been a contented and united family until this young Teddy-boy had wormed his way into her affections.

It was on the tip of his tongue to tell his wife, now, that it was all her fault. She had been the one to say that John

Rockingham wasn't a Teddy-boy, that Judith had met him quite properly at the Tennis Club, and that the boy's father was Chief Metallurgist at the aircraft works; in fact, she'd indicated that, socially, young Rockingham was quite acceptable for Judith.

He'd given his consent to Judith seeing the fellow two or three times a week, chiefly because he had no valid reason for refusing. He knew nothing to the boy's discredit and it was only his own antipathy to him that made him reluctant to accept him as a possible son-in-law.

It was all very well for Judith to tell him that, naturally, he and Rocky didn't have much in common, seeing the vast disparity in their ages. Rocky belonged, like Judith, to the post-war generation, and Harold Bryant was the first to admit that he simply couldn't understand modern youth. He disliked the jeans and sloppy jerseys the boy turned up in. He disliked the casual way he'd look at Judith and say 'Hi!' as if she were of no real importance to him at all. Equally, he disliked the look he'd once or twice caught in the boy's eyes when Judith came into the room where he'd been waiting for her. He'd asked himself once or twice if his was not the reaction of all fathers when their young daughters suddenly grow up and acquire suitors, but he knew it wasn't this alone. Take young Clive Mitchell, at the bank, for instance. Only a junior clerk, but a studious, polite young man determined, as he'd once been himself, to make his way to the top. No jeans and jerseys at the bank, thank you very much. Young Clive was always impeccably turned out. But Judith, shockingly, had called him 'a pompous ass!' She hadn't seemed to appreciate the advantages of a respectable, level-headed young man who might one day make her an excellent husband.

It occurred to him, with a sudden cold shock, that it might be too late now to think of Judith making a good marriage. If it once got round the district that she'd been away with young Rockingham, no matter how innocently she might have behaved, people would still think the worst. Come to that, he'd no reason to be sure that the worst hadn't happened in any case. Why else would they have sneaked off together?

He got up and paced the room furiously. If that young pup had laid a hand on his Judith, he'd murder him. For the first time in his life, he could understand how a man could be driven to physical violence. His wife broke into his thoughts in her thin, anxious voice:

'Perhaps we could ring Mr. and Mrs. Rockingham and find out if the boy's gone, too,' she suggested tentatively. At once, he seized on one of her suggestions with enthusiasm. Action of any sort would be welcome, and it was now nearly seven o'clock. Someone would be sure to be up.

He dialled the number and was relieved that it was Thomas Rockingham, and not his wife, who answered.

Unwilling to spread the news that Judith was gone until he knew for a certainty that this family, too, was involved, he asked for John.

'Rocky? I'm afraid he's not here. Who's speaking, please?'

'Harold Bryant. Could you tell me where I can get hold of your son?'

There was a moment's pause while Thomas Rockingham wondered whether he should mention the strange note Rocky had left behind for them. After all, Harold Bryant was quite an influential person and he might be wrong in supposing it was Bryant's daughter with whom Rocky had gone off. But his wife seemed to have little doubt. And Betsy, Rocky's young sister, had sworn she'd seen Judith in their mother's car on her way home from a friend's house yesterday evening.

Something odd must have happened in the Bryant household to make this man ring him at such an hour of the morning. He decided to take a chance, and as briefly as possible told Harold Bryant of the note left by Rocky.

'So they *have* gone off together!' Bryant said, triumphantly, 'I'm warning you, Rockingham, if your son has so much as laid a finger on my daughter, I shall personally take a horse-whip to him.'

'*If* they have gone off together, then they are both equally to blame,' said Thomas Rockingham calmly. 'And let's get it straight, Mr. Bryant, I've been trying to discourage my son's association with Judith for some time. She's put him right off his work, and my wife and I both feel that she's a bad influence on him. I know Rocky, and he's never been affected by any of his other girl friends. If he's done anything foolish, it's because your daughter egged him on to do it. Do you realize, if there's any scandal the boy could lose his job?'

Bryant's first flush of anger at hearing Judith criticized died as he heard the anxiety in the other man's voice. Himself a logical man, he could see that it was only natural that each family should think the other's was to blame. Of course, Judith was younger, and a girl, but nowadays people didn't seem to consider women as the weaker sex and needing to be looked after and protected. The main thing was to see that no further harm came to her, and this could best be served by keeping on friendly terms with the boy's parents — at least, until both children were safely home again.

As briefly as possible, he explained these sentiments to Rockingham, who was at once in agreement.

'What do you suggest we do, Bryant? Should we call in the police? I'm not anxious for a lot of publicity and I'm sure you're not, either. I don't think I told you they've gone off in my wife's car. I daresay the police could trace them quite easily from the registration number, but, as I say, I don't want it in all the papers.'

'We ought to be able to trace them ourselves. What we've got to decide is where they've gone. Do you think they're trying to get married?'

'I'm pretty sure of it. Rocky thought a lot of your daughter, and she didn't strike me as being the sort of girl who'd just go off with him for a week or two's fun and games. My wife and I have been discussing it most of the night, and we came to the conclusion that if he has Judith with him, they've probably gone to Gretna Green.'

'Gretna!' Harold Bryant echoed the word, annoyed with himself that he hadn't thought of this obvious solution first. If they'd gone there, there was some hope that it wasn't too late to prevent any permanent harm coming from this mad escapade. By law they couldn't get married for three weeks, and somehow he couldn't believe that Judith, with her upbringing, was the kind of girl to disregard convention.

'I'm going straight up there, Rockingham. If they're there, I'll find them and I'll bring Judith home. I don't suppose you want to come with me?'

Rocky's father hesitated. The boy was

twenty, when all was said and done. One couldn't treat him any longer as a child. It was different for the girl's father. She was very much a minor and a good bit younger than his boy. He could imagine himself in Rocky's position, his pride furiously assailed by a parent arriving on the door-step as if he were a school-kid. After all, the last thing he wished to do was to get on bad terms with his son. Ever since the boy had been born, he'd lived for the day when he would take his place in the same factory to which he had devoted his own life. Not to stay at his side, but to go a good deal further, perhaps even in time to become General Manager. He recognized his own limitations but intended that there should be none for Rocky. If that dream was still to come to anything, he must avoid antagonizing his son over this escapade.

'I'm quite prepared to leave it in your capable hands,' he said tactfully. 'You'll let me know any news, of course?'

Half an hour later, Harold Bryant

was driving northwards, his face grim and determined, and his only fear that the young couple had not gone to Gretna after all.

Once, later in the morning, he stopped and telephoned the bank to say he would not be in for a couple of days; and casually, so as not to arouse suspicion, asked his secretary to check Judith's account. It was, as he had thought, closed. She had withdrawn the remainder of her balance at the week-end, thirty-five pounds in all.

He stopped again for lunch and put through a call to each of Gretna's listed hotels. He was a little troubled to hear that in neither place were there people staying in the name of Bryant or Rockingham. His mind quibbled at the thought that they would have registered as Mr. and Mrs. Smith. Judith was too outspoken for deceit. She had always been painfully honest, often getting into trouble in a moment of passion, admitting to a deed which she knew to have been wrong and following it up with 'I don't care.' If she'd chosen to elope with Rockingham, she would do it openly and defy the world, he was sure of it.

But his confidence dwindled a little when he'd scoured the hotels and local boarding houses on his arrival at Gretna, and found no sign of them. He put a call through to Thomas Rockingham, who suggested he might try the garages round about to see if they'd noticed the car. But later that night, he had still found no trace of them so he registered at Rowan Hall and resolved to continue the search next day. To his anxiety for Judith was now added his irritation at being forced to spend the night just over the Border in a nearly-empty hotel. He remembered that he'd arranged two interviews on the morrow, one with an important client and the other with a prospective one whose account he had coveted for some time. He supposed he would have to ring his chief clerk and ask him to postpone both meetings. He was further irritated by his wife's querulous questioning on the telephone, to which he'd been forced to mutter a reassurance which had no foundation in fact.

He did not yet blame Judith for this upheaval in his life. For the time being he attached all the responsibilities to young Rockingham. When he thought of his daughter, which was most of the time, it was with concern for her moral safety. Only once did he consider the fact that he might find her too late, and when he did so he instantly determined that Rockingham should marry her. Then he put the thought away from his mind. Despite all his worries, he was sufficiently tired to sleep soundly that night and did not wake until late next day . . .

*　*　*

When Judith woke, a pale half-hearted sun was streaming through the window of her room and it was a moment or two before she realized where she was.

Then with quickened heart she looked round for Rocky, but found herself alone. When she had entered this room she had welcomed solitude, but now she desperately wanted the reassurance of his presence. Supposing that he'd gone back to England and left her here, alone? She was suddenly quite childishly terrified, and impulsively called his name. A moment or two later she heard his footsteps on the stair, and jumping out of bed she ran to the door and found herself clasped in his strong, young arms. He kissed her fiercely and passionately, almost as if he were trying to draw from her the reassurance she needed from him. He'd just spent an awkward half-hour with the farmer and his wife, who had been questioning him as to how long they would stay. He'd made up some ridiculous story about the car breaking down and then, when they'd enquired where he and his wife were making for, he told them they were merely 'motoring through Scotland'. As if anyone in their right senses would choose December for a motor tour in this bleak countryside. He thought the farmer was shrewd enough to have guessed at the truth, but the simple, kindly woman had taken him at his word and had asked him with a smile if he was on his honeymoon.

'Ye'll no have been married long,' she said with a smile. 'Your wee wife's nae mair than a bairn.'

Rocky looked down into Judith's face and realized how true this was. With her fair hair tumbled about her cheeks, Judith looked hardly a day older than his fourteen-year-old sister Betsy. Downstairs he had felt a cowardly wish to get into the car and drive her home again, and be free of this feeling of responsibility and anxiety, but now as he held her trembling, slender young body in his arms, the same devastating desire to possess her overwhelmed all other thought.

She clung to him tightly, returning his kiss completely reassured by his need for her. This, after all, was why they had come — because Rocky wanted her so much; so that they could be married and become a part of each other's lives. Her tiredness had gone with long, dreamless sleep, and she felt strong and able once more to overcome any barrier ahead of them.

'Oh, Rocky, I do love you so very much. You do know that, don't you, darling?'

He didn't doubt it any more than he doubted his love for her. In this moment he did not doubt, as he often had, that her physical need for him was equal to his own for her. He sensed by the abandonment of her kisses that he could, if he so desired, carry her back to the big bed where he had lain beside her all night, sleeping fitfully, and that she would have made no effort to resist him. But perversely, he could no longer bring himself to take advantage of the moment. It was not that he didn't want her, but because of that momentary resemblance to Betsy. He didn't want to feel responsible for Judith, but in spite of himself he did so.

A little roughly, he pushed her away from him, covering the gesture with a smile.

'Time you got dressed, darling,' he said lightly. 'I've been talking to the farmer and I don't think it's advisable for us to try to stay her for the three weeks. They're getting lunch for us at the moment, and as soon as we've eaten I think we ought to go and find rooms somewhere else. Then I want to put the car in the garage and get it overhauled.'

She didn't question any of these suggestions, happy to acquiesce and fit in with Rocky's easy-going mood which she welcomed with relief after last night's silences.

Impulsively, she stepped towards him and wound her arms round his neck.

'You've no regrets, Rocky? You aren't sorry we came?'

'Of course not, darling. And you?'

'No, no, *no*. I don't mind where I am in the whole world so long as I'm with you, Rocky. I only wish we could be married today. I wish these three weeks were over, and I really was your wife. I don't think I'll be able to believe any of this is real until I can look down and see your ring on my finger.

Rocky grimaced.

'If we're going to pose as man and wife again, I'd better get you a ring right away,' he said, only half-jokingly. 'Haven't you got some kind of ring you can put on for lunch, so they don't notice? What about that garnet ring you sometimes wear? Didn't you bring it with you? You could twist the stone round so only the gold band showed.'

She nodded and went obediently to her suitcase and found the ring, but as she twisted it on to her finger the carefree mood of a moment ago was gone. Although she knew Rocky was sensible to suggest this, she hated the thought of having to deceive the kindly woman who had taken them in so hospitably.

She dressed quickly and hurried downstairs to join Rocky at the farmhouse table, where they had a simple meal of soup, home-cured ham, and apple-pie. The farmer said his wife was busy with the chickens. As soon as they had finished, Rocky paid and they were back once more in the car; this time to drive in daylight along the twisting lanes, back to the village.

'We won't go to a hotel, we'd be too easily traceable. I think we'd better look for rooms,' Rocky said.

And almost immediately he trod on the brakes as they passed a whitewashed cottage with a board, which read: 'Bed and Breakfast.'

'I'll try here,' he told her.

A moment or two later, he was back in the car, his face white and his mouth angry.

'Damned sauce!' he said, shoving the gear in furiously. 'I'd barely opened my mouth to ask for rooms when she said: 'I don't take runaways. There's Mrs. Baddock at the other end of the street. She'll take you, I daresay.''

'Well, at least she told us where to go,' Judith said, trying to console him.

'Besides, she may have been full up or maybe she had a couple who went off without paying the bill.'

Rocky's face relaxed, as she'd hoped it would, but he was still annoyed.

'I hate being made to feel as if I'm doing something *wrong*. This must be it, Judy, she said a grey-stone cottage with a green gate.'

But once inside, Rocky almost wished himself back at the previous place. This woman was quite sickeningly romantic. She gushed round them, like a broody hen with two chicks, calling them 'Poor dears' and asking them innumerable questions, and even seemed to gloat over the prospect that one or other of their parents might come after them. As she led Judith to her room, she poured out an endless monologue on previous elopements she'd been a party to.

'I always put the brides here, the bridegrooms I put in the blue room. More masculine. But he's only across the passage if you need him, dear. Now, if anyone calls and asks for you, am I to say your names or have you an alias you would like me to use?'

Horrified, Judith referred her to Rocky and as quickly as possible closed the door on her. There was something vampire-like about this woman, for all her gushing sweetness. It was as if she were drawing from them nefarious romance, and Judith felt disgusted by the thought that she'd have been pleased if they'd asked for one room instead of two.

She wondered how she would be able to endure the company of such a person for twenty-one days, or was it only twenty, now? It was all right for Rocky, who'd be going off to work, but she'd have to live here. She didn't know if she could stand it without Rocky. Perhaps she, too, could get a job. Anything to get away from those gloating curious eyes.

Rocky, too, must have felt the same way. For the moment her footsteps disappeared down the stairs, he knocked at Judith's door and called:

'Hurry up, Judy. As soon as you're ready I want to get out and find somewhere for the car.'

But they were trapped once more when they got down the stairs by their landlady, Mrs. Baddock.

'Going out again so soon? But of course, you'll be off to see the Smithy. Ever so romantic. Such a pity you can't be married right away, like they could in the old days. Such a shame, I always think. 1856 they stopped it. All sorts of famous people been married there. Earls and lords and noble families by the score. You're in good company, my dears. And don't you worry about anything. If anyone comes for you, I'll say I've never seen you, not either of you . . .'

She was still talking as Rocky pulled the door to behind them.

Subdued, Judith climbed back into the car and felt for Rocky's hand.

'Let's not go back there for tea,' she begged quietly. 'Let's go somewhere ordinary, Rocky. What about the smaller of the two hotels? Rowan Hall.'

He knew it was perhaps silly to acquiesce. The hotels would be the first place her father would search. But at the same time he, too, felt the same need for something 'ordinary', even if it were only stale paste sandwiches and tea in a metal pot.

He stopped at the first garage and asked if they could garage the car and over-haul it. They agreed at once, trade being pretty slack at this time of the year.

'I'll bring it in later this evening,' Rocky said. 'How late could I leave it?'

He was told that it didn't matter. He could leave it in the yard as late as he wished.

Rocky returned to the car, considerably cheered.

'It's all right, darling,' he said. 'We can leave it any time tonight and that means we can drive into Carlisle. There's sure to be a cinema there and it'll take our minds off our worries. We'll ask at the hotel and see what's on.'

Her spirits rose with his. In spite of their dreadful digs, everything was going to be all right. There'd be time enough tomorrow to worry about a job. Meanwhile, Rocky obviously meant that they should enjoy themselves this evening. She was smiling happily as they walked arm-in-arm into the hotel.

3

The phone rang with its usual urgent bell and Gavin Pelham was forced to leave the surgery to answer it. He tried to deal tactfully with a wealthy client who was fussing about her spoilt, over-weight lap-dog, and wished for the hundredth time that morning that Judith was there. As he replaced the receiver with a sigh, he realized that he was only just finding out quite how much of the irksome, administrative tasks she removed from his shoulders.

Of course, this wasn't the first time she'd been away but he had taken his summer holiday at the same time as Judith, so he'd never actually been without her since this time last year when she started to work for him.

Strange to recall, now, that he'd been reluctant to employ her. He'd really wanted a much older, more experienced woman on to whom he could shift the tiresome office side of his practice, leaving him free to deal with the animals. He'd imagined that a mere child of sixteen would be bound to make awkward mistakes, muddle up appointments, and take only a casual interest in the work itself. But, surprisingly, young Judith had settled down and run things for him very efficiently. Only now was he beginning to realize quite how efficiently.

He hurried back into the surgery and continued to treat the black labrador's badly cut pad. He was forced to ask its owner to pass cotton-wool and bandages, and quite naturally the poor man had no idea where to look for them, and once again he found himself missing Judith, not only as a secretary but as a very able assistant.

Working mechanically, his mind pondered the peculiar note he'd received from her yesterday morning. It said, briefly, that circumstances forced her to be away for three weeks, that she deeply regretted she'd been unable to give him prior warning, and could only hope that he would forgive her and hold her job open until her return, although — naturally — she was not counting on such a possibility as she realized how busy he was and how necessary it would be for him to find a replacement. She repeated how sorry she was, how much she enjoyed her work, and thoughtfully added the name of the local Secretarial Bureau where he might find a temporary or permanent replacement. And she ended her note with a promise to explain everything to him as soon as she had time to write.

For twenty-four hours he tried to make sense from Judith's extraordinary behaviour. It was so completely out of character for her to leave him in mid-week, as if he and the job were only of minor importance. His first wave of irritation with her for such inconsiderate behaviour had given way to nagging curiosity. Why, for instance, *three weeks?* If it had been some relation ill, and needing her services, what was there to prevent her telling him the evening before, or even in a very sudden emergency telephoning him and explaining the position? She must know him well enough by now to realize that he would have treated such a request compassionately. It simply didn't make sense.

He had toyed with the idea last night of telephoning her home to demand an explanation, but for some reason he'd been quite unable to explain to himself, he felt he shouldn't do this. And yet his logical mind could provide no reason for this hesitation, and now curiosity was beginning to get the better of him and he decided to ring her house tonight and make enquiries. The fact of the matter was that he didn't want to replace her. He didn't even want a temporary replacement, with the bore of training a new girl to his ways, answering questions and wasting valuable time he could ill afford to lose.

Unless there were some epidemic such as hard-pad, or cat 'flu, he ought to be able to manage on his own for three weeks. After all, he'd coped alone until he decided his practice was sufficiently large to carry a full-time secretarial assistant. But how could he be sure Judith would only be away three weeks? If it were a sick relative, they might need her to stay longer, and with Christmas not so far off he wouldn't be able to cope indefinitely.

He gave the black labrador a kindly pat, told the owner to come back in two days, and showed them out. Back in the surgery, he walked across to the window and stared at his appointments book. Three calls to make this morning. He knew he ought to get started, but still he lingered at the desk, strangely ill-at-ease.

His eyes caught sight of a photograph standing in a neat leather frame behind his blotter. It was of Helen and himself, arm-in-arm at Henley. An enlarged snapshot, really, but so nice of Helen that he'd had it enlarged and framed. He couldn't remember now the man who'd taken the snap, but the evening which followed that exciting afternoon was one he was never likely to forget. It was the first time Helen had indicated she was interested in him. He picked up the frame and studied her face more closely. It was slightly Slav in contour, with high cheekbones, and long, slanting, liquid brown eyes beneath an Edwardian pile of shining black hair, which accentuated the pale olive skin. Even a stranger could have guessed that Helen was a model, if not by her casual elegance then by the way in which she wore her clothes. In the photograph there was a striped blazer slung casually across her shoulders and beneath, a smart, close-fitting linen frock, which seemed to be tapered to that beautiful slender figure — as did all her clothes. He couldn't remember ever seeing Helen look untidy or unkempt, even in the most casual clothes. Small wonder that she turned every male head when she entered a room, and how incredible that she should find him attractive and single him out from all her other admirers.

He looked at his own likeness, seeing that the light-brown hair was blowing across his forehead untidily. It wasn't possible to see the colour of his eyes because they were screwed up against the sun. He thought disparagingly that he looked a good deal older than thirty, but then he'd stopped looking young at eighteen after that year as a prisoner-of-war in the Far East.

His mind shied away, as always, from his disastrous participation in the Korean war. He'd never realized when he started his National Service with such boyish enthusiasm that he was to know only a few weeks' fighting before the other side caught him, and the questioning started . . . He looked back hurriedly at the photograph and tried to see himself through Helen's eyes. There wasn't a man she knew who wasn't crazy about her. Men a good deal better-looking, more influential, richer than he. But she seemed to find him more handsome than the rest, or so she said.

'You remind me of a young Gary Cooper!' she once told him. 'Like a tall, rugged cowboy. There's something about you, Gavin, that I like a lot.'

He didn't know what she meant but it was enough that she'd been willing to let him take her out once or twice in Town and occasionally to some 'do' such as Henley Regatta and Ascot. No doubt she might have let him escort her to other functions if he'd been able to afford to invite her. Thank goodness, he reflected, the practice was doing so well and he was beginning to make a bit more money. But even if things continued like this, it would be some years before he could possibly ask a girl like Helen to marry him.

He replaced the photograph on his desk with a sudden moment of acute depression. It was stupid to kid himself about Helen. In spite of those words at Henley, she wasn't really serious about him — at least, not in the way he would have liked her to be. Ever since he'd met her, he hadn't been able to take a

67

moment's interest in any other woman. But Helen was always out on some date or away for the week-end at some country house whenever he telephoned her. When she returned — and remembered — she would ring him back and tell him she was *longing* to see him, that she missed him *terribly*, that she was far too busy to get down to Yeovil but if he could get up to Town she'd adore to see him. Then, when it was on the tip of his tongue to say he would come up the next weekend, she'd tell him it was an awful bore but she'd promised to go to some house-party or a dance or a theatre, but *please* to ring her again soon.

It was time he stopped fooling himself about Helen. One could hardly see her as the provincial wife of a small-town veterinary surgeon. She'd be bored to tears. Moreover, she hated animals. She'd even given away her miniature peke because she complained it continually shed hairs over her clothes. He knew — had always known — that she wasn't the right wife for him but she fascinated and enthralled him and he couldn't get her out of his mind.

Strange how he always seemed to pick the same type of woman. There was Evelyn, not long after he'd come back from Korea bruised in mind and terribly insecure. He'd needed Evelyn desperately, or perhaps he just needed the comfort and solace of any woman's arms after those ghastly experiences. But Evelyn had been using him to bring the man she really wanted to the point of proposing and, fool that he was, he'd never realized it until she'd walked out and left him, without a backward glance.

He thought of his older sister Rosemary. Plump, matronly, domesticated, a little dull perhaps, but absolutely devoted to her solicitor husband and their three young children. There was nothing mean or unkind or selfish about Rosemary, and presumably there were other women like her in the world. Why couldn't he find someone like her, with whom he could settle down and be happy? He was so often lonely, and he'd have liked kids . . .

He sighed deeply and stood up, squaring his shoulders. He had far too much to do to stay here feeling sorry for himself. Best to take each day as it came and not to think about the past or the future. He'd managed pretty well last year to accept life with a degree of contentment, and it was only this confounded upheaval with Judith that had started him off again, questioning the whys and wherefores, and bringing back that recurring depression he'd thought he had at last got the better of.

He started to pack the hypodermics, forceps and other necessities into his bag when the telephone rang. He toyed with the idea of leaving it unanswered and then realized that it might be an emergency and some poor, dumb animal in dire need of his services, so he turned and lifted the receiver. For a moment or two he couldn't place 'Mrs. Bryant' who was talking to him in a jumbled collection of sentences, and then suddenly realized that this was not a professional call, but Judith's mother.

'I'm so sorry,' he apologized. 'I wonder if you'd repeat what you were saying. I didn't realize who it was.'

'It's about Judith, my daughter, your secretary. My husband thought I ought to ring you and make sure you weren't expecting her in to work. I tried to get you earlier, but your number's been engaged. I'm very sorry, Mr. Pelham. I'm afraid Judith's been a very naughty girl to go off like this. Did she let you know?'

He took advantage of the pause to tell her, briefly, what was in Judith's note.

'I do hope it's nothing serious to have called her away so unexpectedly?'

Olive Bryant had had it deeply impressed upon her by her husband that she must inform none of her friends if they enquired where Judith had gone, or at least where they suspected she had gone. No breath of scandal must leak out for Harold's sake, but she longed to be able to tell someone. Harold had been gone over twenty-four hours, and she was so worried and upset. Surely Mr. Pelham had a right to know what was going on. Besides, when Judith was brought back she'd need something to occupy her mind and Mr. Pelham might feel more kindly disposed towards her when he realized that the three weeks would be curtailed to a few days. Judith loved her job, and the poor child would be unhappy enough, without losing that interest on top of everything else.

Gavin listened, with as much patience as he could, to the garbled story Olive Bryant gave. It sounded so utterly improbable that he wondered for one moment whether the poor woman was in her right mind. He couldn't think who she meant when she mentioned 'Rocky'. As far as he knew, Judith hadn't any regular boy friend, but then he'd never really taken an interest in her life outside the practice.

An elopement to Gretna Green! He

realized suddenly that this explained the puzzling 'three weeks'; a 'minor' could get married in Scotland provided she had resided there for twenty-one days. But why couldn't Judith have been married from her own home? Obviously, this 'Rocky' Mrs. Bryant kept mentioning was an undesirable type they didn't wish her to marry. Or more likely, they felt she was too young and, of course, they would be right. What could a child of seventeen, not long left school, possibly know about life and love, and the world in general! How appallingly ignorant he'd been at that age. He remembered himself the year before he'd been called up, as a mere schoolboy; and yet, there was something strangely mature about Judith, for all her youthful appearance. The way she ran the administrative side of his practice, her sense of responsibility, and the tactful way she dealt with the more trying clients, such as Mrs. Campbell-Fox with that over-fed dachshund of hers!

He pulled himself together and told the distraught mother that he would certainly keep the job open for Judith, that she must try not to worry, and that no doubt her husband would have Judith safely home again before nightfall. Would she be kind enough to keep him informed, as naturally he was concerned.

He put down the phone and hurried out to his car, realizing he was well behind schedule. At least it was something of a relief to think that he wasn't going to have to manage without Judith for as long as she had inferred in her note. He hoped her father would find her and bring her home before long, and then with a sudden feeling of compassion for the young elopers he wondered if she was going to be desperately unhappy. He tried to imagine how he would feel, keyed up no doubt, and swept along on a wave of romantic emotion. It was going to be a bit of an anticlimax to be dragged home by papa, put back to work, and told to behave yourself, like a naughty child.

He wondered if the slightly hysterical Mrs. Bryant would be able to handle the psychological needs of her daughter, once she returned. He'd not met the father, but quite obviously he wasn't a man who believed in *laissez faire*.

A picture of Judith's pale, serious little face flashed momentarily into his mind and was gone again. What a hell of a world this was for everyone! Only people like Rosemary seemed to be able to find peace and happiness. Perhaps it was something in the temperament a person was born with that gathered in the good, happy things of life, and without knowing it warded off the heartbreak, the disillusion and the evil. And perhaps the wretched little Judith was destined to be another like himself, longing for Rosemary's kind of life and yet standing always on the fringe of it. When she came back, he would try to make things as easy as possible for her, take an interest in her. She'd probably need a shoulder to cry on, and it was time he'd forgot his own worries and concerns and thought about someone else.

He pulled up at the large farm-house, which was his first call, and realized that Mrs. Bryant had lifted a load off his mind. By tomorrow, or the next day, Judith would be home and life would be back to normal.

He forgot her, as he gave his mind completely to the job in hand.

4

Harold Bryant felt highly satisfied with the way things were going. After a good night's rest he decided to tackle the new day in a calm and logical fashion. First, to enquire in person at the hotels if they'd seen anyone answering Judith's or Rockingham's description, then at the boarding houses, and finally the garages. Sooner or later, he must inevitably find them since they couldn't remain hidden indefinitely.

Now with this first enquiry at the smaller of the two hotels, he'd learned that a young couple answering his description had had tea there yesterday afternoon. On receipt of a ten-shilling note, the hall-porter recalled that they'd driven away in a rather battered Morris car in the direction of Carlisle, and that if they were hoping to be married at Gretna they would most likely be staying with Mrs. Baddock at number 35 Hamilton Terrace.

He left the hotel and drove towards the address given to him, feeling reasonably confident that he'd tracked Judith down. Not, he told himself, that he ever doubted his ability to do so. He hadn't been made manager of the Amalgamated Bank for nothing. Sound commonsense was the answer to any problem and that was one thing he'd always been able to apply.

His self-confidence was a trifle shaken when the voluble Mrs. Baddock opened the door to him and informed him that she had no such couple staying. She was chatty, and over-friendly, and he distrusted her. But, fortunately, her desire to elaborate tripped her up. When for the third time she told him that she hadn't seen any 'fair young lady with a page-boy bob', he knew she was lying. He had described his daughter as young and fair, but he certainly hadn't mentioned her hair-style. Almost immediately he heard Judith's voice, and he pushed roughly past Mrs. Baddock and went to the foot of the stairs.

'Come down here this minute, Judith,' he called, without waiting to ascertain that it was really her. He heard a door bang on the landing above, and the sound of a key turning in the lock, and went as quickly as his portly frame would allow, to the top of the stairs.

'Judith, I know you're in there. Come out this minute!'

She spoke to him in a quiet, determined voice.

'I'm sorry, Father, but I'm not coming. Not if you wait there all day and all night. I'm not coming out, Father, so please don't make a fuss.'

'Is Rockingham in there with you?' he demanded.

'No, he's not, Father. He's not in the house or even in Gretna. I've told you that I'm not coming out. I'm going to marry Rocky, and nothing you can say or do will stop me.'

'You'll do as I say — ' Mr. Bryant

broke off, abruptly, realizing that this was perhaps not the best way to deal with the position. Perhaps Judith wasn't aware of the legal side. Since she was still a minor, he had control over her movements and if necessary he could call on the law to force her to submission.

'Look here, Judith,' he said in a more reasonable tone. 'Whatever we have to say to each other can at least be said in private. If you won't come out, then you might at least let me come in.'

A moment or two later the key turned in the lock and Judith cautiously opened the door. Seeing he was alone, she opened it wider, and let him come in, closing the door behind him. He glanced quickly round the room, noting that there was only one bed, and that there was no sign that young Rockingham had been here. Involuntarily, he said aloud:

'Thank God I'm not too late.'

Judith looked at her father, an angry colour flaring into her cheeks. No doubt he had fully anticipated 'the worst'. It reduced the love she had for Rocky, and his for her, to a level which could only offend her idealistic mind. She walked over to the window and stared miserably out at the row of terraced houses. At least she could be glad that Rocky had left early this morning on the bus to Carlisle, in the hope of finding a job. He'd been spared this embarrassment, if nothing else. She flung her head back and faced her father, defiantly.

'It's no good, Father. Nothing you can say will make me change my mind. I love Rocky, and he loves me, and we want to be married.'

He sat down on the bed and glanced at his daughter irritably. Couldn't the silly girl see for herself that she was making a hopeless mess of her life? How old was Rockingham? Not yet twenty-one, and only an apprentice to boot. What kind of life would Judith have with him? Why, they wouldn't even be able to afford their own home for years to come.

He tried, calmly, to make her see this,

but Judith seemed blind to reason.

'Do you think I care?' she asked him, angrily. 'We know we'll probably have to live in furnished rooms, but so long as we are together we won't mind, and you don't have to worry we're counting on you or Rocky's parents to help us. We don't need your help. I shall keep on working, and we shall manage quite well.'

'And suppose you start a family?' her father said, bluntly. 'I suppose you never thought of that?'

'We don't plan to have children until Rocky's well established,' Judith said, trying to be reasonable and make him see her point of view.

'All the same, mistakes can happen, and then where would you be? I'm not going to allow it, Judith. Quite apart from anything else, I don't think Rockingham would make you a suitable husband.'

'How can you know what I want!' Judith flared at him. 'It's I who will be marrying him, Father, and living with him, not you. We aren't living in the

Victorian era any more, you know. And nowadays people marry for love, and not because their parents wish it or think it a good match,' she ended scornfully.

'All the same, my girl, you'd do well to remember that you're still a minor, and for the time being, anyway, what I say goes.'

Once again he tried to curb his impatience and to keep his voice on a more reasonable level.

'Now look here, Judith, I don't want you to think I've come all this way just to spite you. You've never found me unreasonable before. If you're fair, you'll admit that I've never refused you anything you wanted, within reason. I even agreed to your going on seeing Rockingham, in spite of my distrust of him. This — this elopement has only proved to me how right my instinct was. I think he's quite irresponsible, to say the least of it, and I'd have liked him a good deal better if he'd at least had the guts to come and ask my permission to marry you before deciding to elope with you.'

'That's not fair!' Judith defended Rocky. 'Rocky's no fool and we both knew you would never give your consent. You've no right to say he was afraid to face you. The only reason we didn't ask was because we knew it would be pointless. And what reason have you got for calling Rocky irresponsible? He didn't *make* me come here with him. We decided together.'

'And I've decided that you're coming home with me,' said Harold Bryant, standing up, tight-lipped and angry. 'And I'm telling you again, Judith, that if you won't come voluntarily, I shall make you. And if you really do love this boy, you'll think twice about forcing my hand. If I have to call in the police, the whole sordid affair will come out and he'll lose his job. I'm not without influence in the district, and I shan't hesitate to put the full blame on him. It so happens that three of the directors of his firm bank with me, and they won't be anxious to take Rockingham's part against me. I'll give you half-an-hour to think it over. Meanwhile, I shall go down and wait in the car.'

A little of Judith's bravado vanished as her father's footsteps receded down the stairs. If only Rocky were here to advise her what to do! She was not going home, not until she was Rocky's wife and had a right to share his life. If only she were a little more sure of the legal position; she knew her father well enough to be sure that he was fully conversant with his rights as a parent. The phrase 'Ward of the Court' came into her head, and she supposed that in emergencies such as this he would be able to take legal action before the three weeks expired. Their only hope would be for Rocky and herself to disappear again, and how were they to do this? The car was in dock, and even if they were to go by bus her father only had to wait at the corner of the road and follow them.

She was suddenly appalled by the undignified and humiliating position in which they stood. Rocky was going to hate it. It wasn't fair of her father to call Rocky a coward, but nevertheless he *did* avoid her father whenever it was possible. Not because he was afraid of him, she was sure, but because he knew her father disapproved of him. If Rocky had been a weak, spineless creature, he would never have dared to defy everyone to bring her here. Her father would call it 'running away', but to her and Rocky it was putting up a fight for what they believed to be right.

If only she had somebody to talk to, someone to advise her how best to get out of this predicament.

As if in answer to her thoughts, there was a knock on the door and Mrs. Baddock peered round into the room and said, conspiratorially:

'He's still outside in his car. It's your father, isn't it? I tried to tell him you weren't here but he seemed quite sure that you were. And then, bless your heart, you started to sing, you poor wee thing, and he recognized your voice. Such a shame, two nice souls like you and the young gentleman. I suppose your father will make you go home? Of course, there is a back door; I could let you out there and you could leave a message with me for the young gentleman to say where you'd gone.'

'She's enjoying it,' Judith thought with disgust. 'I bet this is just the sort of situation she anticipates when she takes in couples like us. Tomorrow she'll be able to tell all her neighbours about it, and they'll listen and envy her for having been in on it all.'

'Please go. I want to be alone.' Her voice was raised a little hysterically. She tried to calm herself, and said more quietly: 'Please, Mrs. Baddock, I need to be by myself to think.'

With a look of chagrin the woman departed, leaving Judith even further dismayed. The thought of Mrs. Baddock covering her departure through the back door was utterly repugnant to her, and yet, what alternative was there? To go back with her father now, and then make another attempt later? She wasn't sure she could stand it. The last forty-eight hours had not been exactly fun for either of them, and what chance had they of succeeding any better next time? And how could she go, leaving Rocky to come back to the empty house, with only that revolting Mrs. Baddock to tell him what happened? It would be such a terrible disappointment to him. Last night in the car, on their way back from the cinema, he'd kissed her again and again, telling her how desperately he needed her, wanted her, and that he lived only for the moment when he could really at long last call her his wife.

Last night it had really seemed possible that their dreams would come true. Nineteen days to go, and after that no one could ever come between them again. It seemed fantastic to Judith that she'd never taken seriously the thought that her father would guess where they had gone, and follow them. They hadn't covered their tracks very well.

Judith had still not come to a decision when her father knocked on the door once more, and she let him in.

'Well, are you coming, Judith?' He seemed to take it for granted that she would.

Poor old Daddy! He looked so worried and upset. He was only acting in what he believed to be her interests. If only she could make him understand that Rocky was wonderful, and so much more right for her than that horrible, pompous Clive Mitchell at the bank. She'd have died of boredom, married to such a 'worthy' young man. Surely her father could see it, too.

She turned to him and held out her hand in appeal.

'Please, Daddy!' She unconsciously used the childish term. 'Won't you let me stay here and marry Rocky? I do love him. I shall never love anyone else. Even if you were to force me to come home, it wouldn't do any good because I shall marry him in the end. If it's the elopement you object to, I'm quite prepared to come back with you and be married in the church at home. I'd far rather. We'd both prefer it. If you'll only give your permission, and promise, I'll come home with you now, this minute.'

But he wouldn't. He was a man of principles and he'd always lived and acted according to what he believed to be right. His attitude to Judith's 'escapade' could be summed up quite simply. In the first place, she was far too young to be married to anyone. In the second place, she was far too inexperienced to judge for herself what was necessary for a life-partner and, lastly, he did not approve of young Rockingham. It would therefore be quite wrong to let Judith believe he was willing to give his consent to their marriage if she would come home of her own free will, and it never occurred to him to deceive her.

'I'm sorry, Judith, but I couldn't even permit an official engagement. The furthest I can go is to say that I won't stop your seeing him. It's my belief that in a year or two, you'll think quite differently about him, and I feel it's my duty to let you have those two years in which to come to your senses.'

She knew in that moment that it was useless either to plead or argue with him. When her father spoke of 'doing his duty', there was no moving him.

Distraught, she cried aloud:

'But I can't go back, Father. I *must* marry him.'

For the first time, a little of Harold Bryant's complacency deserted him. Because it had never been far from the back of his mind, he was all too ready to misinterpret her words.

'*Must* . . . .' Then he was too late after all. He looked at her white face in horrified concern.

'You, Judith, my daughter, of all people — ' he broke off, too embarrassed by the situation to continue.

It was Judith's turn to look back at her father, horrified, as she realized the wrong conclusion he had drawn from her words. Her pride was desperately hurt, and it was as if he had soiled her beautiful relationship with Rocky by his horrible suspicions. Hurt, she sought for words to hurt him back and was stung to reply:

'I suppose if I were going to have Rocky's child, you'd be pushing me up the aisle, instead of trying to drag me away from him.'

Her young, clear voice was full of scorn.

'Then it wouldn't matter what Rocky was like, provided he made an honest woman of me and you didn't have to tell all your important clients that your daughter was having an illegitimate child. Then it would be your *duty* to ensure he did marry me. Old people are all the same. You're hypocrites. You wouldn't be capable of understanding what love really means . . . '

She broke off and flung herself down on the bed in a torrent of angry, humiliated tears. Her father looked down at her in a mixture of embarrassment and perplexity. Was he to understand that there was no urgent need of this wedding after all? If so, he owed his daughter an apology. He wished his wife were here to deal with Judith in this moment. Not that he could believe Olive would be able to cope much better than he. One hysterical female was quite enough, he thought irritably. At the same time, there was such a hopeless, despairing quality in Judith's tears, that his quite genuine love for her prompted him to put an arm round her shoulders.

She shook it off as if his touch were repulsive to her, and destroyed the moment of compassion. Irritated once more, he said:

'Now that's enough of that, Judith. Get your suitcase packed. If we start at once we can be home before midnight.'

Judith sat up, her tear-streaked face raised defiantly to him.

'Nothing will make me leave here until I've spoken to Rocky,' she said in a small, flat voice. 'You don't think I'd walk out and leave him without even saying goodbye, do you?'

He sensed a weakening in her resolve and pressed home his advantage quickly:

'I'm quite prepared to let you say goodbye to Rockingham,' he said reasonably. 'Where is he?'

'He's in Carlisle, looking for a job. I doubt very much whether he'll be back before tea-time.'

'Then you'd better come back to my hotel and have some lunch with me,' her father said. 'We've a lot of things to discuss. One thing we'll have to decide is what we're going to tell the people who ask about your sudden disappearance. We'd better all tell the same story.'

'I don't want any lunch and I'm not going to discuss anything until I've spoken to Rocky,' she said quietly.

Seeing his hesitation, she added sarcastically: 'Since you don't trust me not to run away again, you can lock me in if you wish. I've no intention of leaving this room until Rocky comes back.'

'Don't be silly, Judith. I'm quite prepared to accept your word. Have I your promise?'

She nodded her head, mutely.

'I'd like to see Rocky alone, please,

Father. After I've spoken to him, I'll ring you at your hotel, I promise.'

'Very well then, Judith. I'm staying at Rowan Hall. I shall expect you to ring me before seven.'

There was nothing more to say, and avoiding each other's eyes they parted company, Judith to return to her bed in helpless immobility, and Bryant to return to his hotel more than a little perturbed and without any of his earlier elation at having so easily traced his daughter.

Disregarding the cost, he put through a call to his wife to reassure her and tell her he would probably be driving through the night, and reach home in time for breakfast.

'I'm afraid Judith's going to be a bit upset,' he warned his wife. 'I should think it a good idea not to ask too many questions unless she seems willing to confide in you.'

He went back into the hotel lounge and ordered himself a double whisky.

Rocky got off the bus and turned into

Hamilton Terrace with misgivings. He dreaded the thought of that awful Mrs. Baddock opening the door to him, as much as he dreaded the thought of having to wipe the happy expectancy off Judith's face. He'd had no luck at all in getting a job in Carlisle. The first two places he'd been to had no vacancy, and the third had asked for a reference and insurance card, neither of which he could produce. The obvious place to go was the Labour Exchange, but he'd been forced to realize that they, too, would probably ask for references and details about his former employment, and to give these would lead to their hide-out being discovered if Judith's father had reported her absence to the police. If it weren't for the fact that he wanted Judith more than ever, he'd have been inclined to throw in his hand and take her home himself. These last two days had been pretty ghastly one way and another. But Judy hadn't once complained and she had so much more courage than he. He wouldn't give up, as long as she was willing to go through with it. They had enough money between them to last these three weeks without a job, and once back in England he could always get work even if his firm refused to accept his absence without leave.

He was totally unprepared for the news Mrs. Baddock hastened to give him as she opened the door to his knock. He pushed past her and ran up the stairs to Judith's room. As he opened the door, she ran into his arms, the tears pouring down her cheeks as she sobbed his name over and over again. He managed to calm her after a moment or two, but she clung fiercely to his arm as if only by doing so could she feel secure.

'It's no good, Rocky. Father isn't going to give his consent and, knowing him, he's quite capable of parking the car outside this house until I do go back with him. What are we going to do, Rocky? I can't go home. I *can't!*'

Rocky thought of his prospective

father-in-law with dismay. Despite his dislike of Harold Bryant, he was forced to respect him as a man not to be lightly persuaded against what he believed to be his duty. One could, in all honesty, see his point of view. Judith was only a kid and he, Rocky, had damn little to offer her. Nothing at all, if it came to that. He mightn't even have a job, for all he knew. And Judith was an only child.

Judith seemed to sense his thoughts, for she was staring now into his face as if he could perform some magic that would put everything right again.

'You're not going to let him take me home, Rocky? Please, darling, *please*!'

He knew there was nothing he could do. They could refuse to go, and Bryant could go to law and have Judith made a Ward of Court. He would then be in Contempt of Court, if he disobeyed the order and married her. The whole world was against them, and one couldn't fight the whole world. Unable to offer her any hope, he was forced to turn away from her and the desperate look in her eyes.

But she wouldn't give up so easily.

'There must be something we can do, Rocky. I gave my word to Father that I wouldn't leave this house without telling him, but he'll be back soon and we could face him together. He can't *force* me to get in the car and go home with him, and perhaps we could disappear somehow. Other couples have. It's in the papers every day.'

Her voice trailed away doubtfully as she saw no answering eagerness in Rocky's face. She caught hold of his arms and forced him to look at her.

'Rocky, you do still love me, don't you? You do still want us to be married?'

Of course, he did, but the situation had got out of control, and he wasn't sure he felt capable of prolonging the fight against such overwhelming odds. It was all very well for Judith to talk about fleeing to the Highlands, but she seemed to have forgotten that they had no car, very little money and only the slimmest chance of getting away with it. Perhaps he knew Harold Bryant's type better than Judith. In a way they were rather alike. Once they made up their minds it would take a great deal to deter them from pursuing a course of action they had chosen. Odd, really, because Judith with her fair, pale beauty and her childish appearance gave no indication of this inner strength and determination. He envied her at this moment her single-mindedness. Perhaps it was the extra three years that made him, alone, appreciate the difficulties that would lie ahead of them. Or was he just weak?

He stared down at Judith's pale face streaked with the tears she had shed earlier, and no longer beautiful. Of course, he did love her as much as ever, but surely it would be better to comply now with her father's wishes and then make fresh plans when a new opportunity arose.

'Darling, you could perhaps come to an understanding with your father. You could tell him that you'll go back with him now, so long as he gives his word he won't prevent us from seeing each other as much as we want in the future. He'll be sure to agree, since his alternative would be to take legal proceedings and I'm sure in his position he won't want to do that unless he's forced to it. He might even agree to an engagement and then maybe we could be married next year.'

She turned away from him, suddenly so exhausted with emotion that she was incapable of fighting further. Unless Rocky wanted to go through with this as much as she did, she might as well go home. Perhaps Rocky could see things more clearly than she did. She couldn't think straight any more.

'All right!' she said flatly. 'I'll go.'

He knew now that this was the end of the elopement. Judith would go back with her father and he would follow her in a day or two when the car was ready. And now that he was so close to parting from her, he wanted her again. He felt angry with her for having wasted these last two nights which they could so easily have spent in each other's arms. At least they would have had this memory to take away with them and he wouldn't be feeling this bitter frustration. It was Judith's old-fashioned persistence that they should be married before they made love that had brought them to a ridiculous position. If they could have belonged to each other physically, they could have waited to get married. It was only because they wanted each other so much that they'd come here. But obviously, Judith's need for him did not match his desire for her or she wouldn't have kept him at arm's length all these months. Even now, when they still had an hour alone together, he sensed that her answer would still be 'no'. Perhaps she wasn't really to blame. In some ways she was so young, and having parents who were nearer the age of his grandparents, it stood to reason that she'd been brought up strictly. In one way, her innocence was one of the things that attracted him to her.

He knew by the desperately unhappy look in her face that he ought to go to her and comfort her with kisses, but he couldn't bring himself to touch her. He might not be able to keep himself under control . . .

Judith began to pack, her face turned away from him now so that he couldn't see the tears that were pouring down her cheeks. If only Rocky would take her in his arms and kiss her, it wouldn't be so bad, but he was standing by the window with an angry scowl on his face and she couldn't help feeling that he was blaming her for the way things had turned out. She loved him more than ever. So much, in fact, that if he were to touch her now, she knew that there would be no resistance left in her. She wanted to belong to him with a new desperation. If they couldn't be married, at least their physical union would be something to bind them together, to remember when she was home again, to give point and reason to these last two days.

She wasn't sufficiently experienced to understand her feelings for what they really were. She sensed that he was withdrawing from her and in her unconscious mind she knew that her physical surrender would bring him back to her.

But it was too late.

'I'm not going to stay and create a scene with your father,' Rocky was saying, 'I think it's best all round if I disappear for a while, Judith. I'll get in touch with you the moment I get home.'

He went to her now, putting his arms round her and touching the back of her head in a brief farewell kiss. He felt her shoulders shaking beneath his touch and knew that she was crying. For a moment, he felt strangely close to tears himself.

He turned abruptly from her, and a moment later he was gone.

5

Two days later, Judith returned to work. Gavin Pelham was delighted to see her, but appalled by the white, ravaged little face. He was moved to say impulsively:

'Are you sure you're all right, Judith? I can quite well manage Saturday on my own.'

She tried to control the stinging tears that seemed so ready now to rush to her eyes when anyone spoke to her kindly. Gavin Pelham least of all had reason to be kind to her. She'd been more than grateful to hear from her mother that he was keeping the job open.

'I'm quite all right, thank you. I'd rather be working — ' She broke off, unable to continue, and busied herself putting on the white nylon coat she always wore in the surgery.

He stood undecidedly watching her.

Poor little thing! She looked as if she hadn't slept for nights and he wondered whether her father had given her a rough time of it. He found himself wondering, too, what would happen now. Would she be allowed to go on seeing the boy? Surely in this day and age her parents would handle the situation tactfully. Anyone with the slightest knowledge of psychology would know that separation of that sort was bound to aggravate the desire rather than induce indifference.

Of course, it was none of his business, he told himself. And yet, as the morning wore on, and Judith worked efficiently but without any of her usual brisk enthusiasm, he felt more and more concerned about her. He couldn't fail to notice that every time the phone rang, her face would come alive and she would rush towards the desk expectantly, and leave it a moment or two later in mute despair. It was so obvious that she must be expecting to hear from the boy-friend. Despite himself, he began to listen for the phone and to catch something of her own hope and consequent despair. Why in heaven's name didn't the young fool ring her, and wipe that look from her face? He knew what it was like, waiting for the loved one to ring. How many times had Evelyn promised to call him at six, and failed to do so? How many times had he stood with his hand on the receiver, fighting the desire to ring her, and knowing all too well that if he did so it would only be to find she was out with 'the other man'? Thank God his feelings for Helen had never come to that pitch. He'd never allowed himself to believe that she really loved him, or that there was any real hope that she would marry him.

Perhaps this desperate belief that what one desired so deeply must come about, belonged only to the very young. The years brought a cynical acceptance of the truth, that only seldom in life did things work out the way one wanted them to. No, it wasn't easy being young. He wouldn't want to go through the process of growing-up again.

He knew it was Judith's custom to lunch at a small café down the road. His daily woman would have left his own lunch ready — something that would keep warm in the oven in case he was late back from a call. But the thought of the girl sitting alone in that rather shabby tea-shop, in her present frame of mind, moved him to say:

'I've got a call to make the far side of Yeovil and I may need some help. There's a rather bad-tempered billy-goat and I've been called in to cut his horns. I may need you to keep him still while I do the job. We could lunch in Yeovil on the way back, if that's all right with you?'

He made the invitation as casual and as impersonal as possible, not wishing to seem to intrude in any way on her private misery. She acquiesced at once, without enthusiasm, and he knew it really didn't matter to her one way or the other. She was trying to keep herself under control, but as the hours went by he felt that sooner or later she was going to break.

By mid-afternoon there were dark rings beneath her eyes and she had made two quite serious mistakes on his appointments pad. In one case, filling a visit in for the wrong day, and in another writing the wrong name. Normally, he would not have been paying attention to her conversations on the phone, but because he felt so concerned for her he found himself listening even while he worked at the little cupboard which served as his dispensary. He was wondering whether to mention it to her, as she handed the book to him at the end of the day, but quite suddenly she saw the second mistake herself, and grabbing the book away from him, almost rudely, took it back to the desk and started to erase the name frantically with a rubber. A moment later, her head went down on her arm and she was crying uncontrollably.

Unlike a lot of men who are embarrassed by a woman's tears, Gavin was more than competent to deal with the situation. It was this instinct for another's feelings that perhaps made him such a good vet and so popular with his sister's children. Normally rather shy, perhaps even introverted, he was able now to go across to Judith and quite simply offer her the comfort of his shoulder to weep on. He stroked the shining, gold head, gently and rhythmically, the way he might have soothed a nervous pony or quietened a restless child.

Slowly, Judith grew calmer. She was surprised to find that there seemed nothing strange about her being here, with Gavin's arms round her, with the comforting doggie smell of his tweed jacket beneath her cheek. She was making an utter fool of herself, and yet it didn't seem to matter. In fact, nothing seemed to matter very much any more. It was such a relief to have reached this insensibility. If only it could last, that she could stay here for ever and ever, and never care about anything any more.

He was talking to her now, and she tried to concentrate on what he said.

'You mustn't mind so much, Judith. Whatever it is that's hurt you, it won't go on hurting you, believe me. Everything bad comes to an end, in the end. It will all come right, you'll see.'

'But it can't come right,' Judith said, sniffing like a small girl. He handed her a clean white handkerchief, and she blew her nose gratefully and added in a choked little voice:

'At least, not for years and years.'

She moved away from him and sat down in her chair at the desk, her back towards him.

'Would you care to talk about it? Sometimes it helps to confide in someone.'

She turned her head and smiled at him, tearfully, suddenly liking him very much indeed. He was right. It would be such a relief to be able to talk to someone quite impartial. For the last forty-eight hours she had to listen to her father's condemnation of Rocky and her mother's hysterical questioning as to what she had done. And no word from Rocky. She didn't even know whether he was in Scotland or England. She wasn't even sure whether he loved her any more.

Calmly now, she gave Gavin a brief outline of the last few days. Surprisingly he found himself rather in agreement with Judith's father. If Gavin had been in Rockingham's shoes, he wouldn't have let anything come between himself and the girl he loved; but then it was always easy to say something like that when one wasn't faced with the situation oneself. Maybe it took more courage to give up the girl you loved, than to run away with her again. But surely the boy could have mustered enough courage to stay and plead with Bryant. Who knows, Judith's father might have weakened and given his consent at the last moment. But it was obvious from everything Judith had said that Bryant didn't consider the boy the right husband for Judith. He must have other reasons besides the fact that the boy was only on the threshold of his career.

'You say your father has agreed to your going on seeing this boy. If that's so, things aren't too hopeless, are they?' he said, reasonably. 'Your father must realize that you could both go to Court and might obtain the Magistrates' permission to get married, despite his own disapproval, unless of course your father knows something to Rocky's discredit.'

Judith shrugged her shoulders.

'Rocky's just not Father's type. He wants me to marry someone dull, like Clive Mitchell. I think Father believes Rocky is some kind of glorified Teddy-boy. The awful thing is that I don't think my father is really concerned with my happiness at all. He admitted that if I . . . ' she hesitated suddenly ' . . . why, well, what I mean is, if I *had* to marry Rocky he would be the *first* one to insist on an immediate wedding, no matter what he thought of Rocky. The only thing he minds is that his respectable friends shouldn't be shocked,' she ended bitterly.

He took her up on these words quickly, seeing a fresh way to comfort her and lighten her depression.

'If that's so, Judith, all is not lost is it? In the last resort, you and your young man hold the trump card. You know now that you can always force your father's consent!'

She actually managed to smile.

'I never thought of that. Oh, I *do* wish Rocky would phone.'

He smiled back at her and said gently:

'It's rather like the watched pot never boiling. The moment you stop listening for the phone, it will ring. In fact, I think it would be a good idea if you keep as far as possible from the sound of the bell. What about coming to a cinema with me tonight? I believe the local's doing a revival of 'Doctor In The House', and it would do you good to laugh. I'd like to see it again, too.'

'You're being wonderfully kind to me,' Judith said gratefully. 'I think I would enjoy the film. At least, it would be better than another night at home with Father glowering at me, and Mummy flapping round like a mother-hen with a lost chick.'

'That is what friends are for, to help in emergencies,' he said, and realized suddenly that Judith would never be just his secretarial assistant again. Child though she was, he liked to think that she was now his friend, and if he could ever help her at all it would make him happy to do so. She was such a guile-less, innocent little thing, really, and there was something which touched him about the quiet, unreserved quality of her love for this boy. So unlike Helen, who gave with one hand and took away with the other. He only hoped that the boy was worth all this heart-break and anxiety and was worthy of her.

After she had gone home for an early supper and to change before the film, Gavin sat and pondered the outcome of Judith's rather crazy and fruitless elopement. There was absolutely no doubting her love for the boy she'd run away with, but what about his love for her? Despite Judith's defence of him, Gavin had the uneasy feeling that something was wrong. Even the most unintuitive lover must know what Judith was going through at this moment, the anticlimax and feeling of frustration. Surely Rockingham could have found a moment to telephone her! He must know the number of the surgery, even if he didn't wish to phone her home.

Gavin shrugged his shoulders in sudden, amused surprise. This was ridiculous. He was beginning to feel as tense as Judith, anticipating this phone call. No doubt the boy had his reasons and he, poor devil, couldn't be feeling any too happy, either.

He was both surprised and immensely pleased for Judith's sake when she met him later outside the cinema, her face radiant with happiness.

'He rang me!' she said at once, breathlessly. 'Just after I got back. Of course, we couldn't say much, the phone's in the drawing-room at home and I was able to warn Rocky that Mother and Father were both listening. But he told me he'd got the car and would be driving back from Scotland tonight. He'll be home tomorrow morning.'

She smiled up at him in spontaneous delight.

'Oh, Gavin. I'm so happy now and you were quite right — about the kettle, I mean. When the phone rang, I thought it was probably you to tell me you'd made a mistake about the time, or something. I wasn't expecting it to be Rocky, and it was such a wonderful surprise.'

He took her arm and pressed it gently against his side. He felt happy, too. He wasn't quite sure if it was just that her own good spirits were infectious or the knowledge that she must have accepted him as a friend, since for the first time during the months he'd known her she had called him by his Christian name.

6

'It was very decent of your mother to let you have the car this evening, after last week,' Judith said warmly.

Rocky had picked her up at the surgery and was now driving out of the town so that they could park the car and discuss all the thousands of things they had to say to one another. When he'd rung the surgery bell just after six o'clock, her heart had leapt into her throat and she'd longed to rush to the door and fling herself into Rocky's arms. It seemed so much, much longer than one week since they'd parted so wretchedly in that horrible room at Gretna! But because of Gavin's presence, they'd merely glanced at one another briefly and Judith had introduced the two men, suddenly strangely anxious that Gavin should like Rocky. Gavin had proved a wonderful friend these last few days, never prying into the deep privacy of her thoughts but somehow making her aware that she could confide in him whenever she wished and that if it were possible he would try to help her. Maybe she'd found it so much easier to talk to him than to her parents because, although years older than herself, he was much closer to her generation than they were.

She recalled her parents' faces when, the night before, she'd announced that she had arranged to meet Rocky after work this evening. There'd been a shocked silence and a look of protest on her father's face, which had forced her to say quickly:

'You haven't forgotten, Father, that you promised to let me go on seeing Rocky if I came back with you of my own free will?'

She knew her father regretted the promise but he couldn't go back on it and the most he could do was to tell her sternly that she must be in by midnight or else he might have to rescind his word.

As if in tune with her thoughts about her family, Rocky said suddenly:

'There was the most ghastly fuss at home this morning. When I told them I wouldn't be in to supper they guessed I was meeting you, and then it all started up again — 'Can't you see you're ruining your career?' — on and on until I thought I would go crazy. Dad never stops reminding me that it was only due to him that the firm has kept me on and I suppose he's right, but if he says it once more I shall do something desperate.'

He turned the car into a side road and pulled up on the kerb, switching off the headlamps. The next moment he had caught her roughly in his arms and was kissing her with a violence that frightened her. His mouth was pressed against her own so tightly that she felt only pain. She struggled against him, startled and a little afraid of him. There was no tenderness in him at this moment. It seemed to her as if he were angry with her and wanting to hurt her.

She managed to struggle free and protested weakly. But he paid no attention to her small cry or the feeble pressure of her hands against his chest, and began to kiss her once more as if determined to bend her to his will.

Her uncertainty gave way to fear. What was the matter with Rocky? He seemed quite beyond control. Strangely, her own mind was perfectly calm as she tried to think how best to cope with a situation she could never have anticipated.

'I've got to have you, Judy,' Rocky was saying, over and over again, his voice rough and unrecognizable.

'Not this way,' she thought, desperately trying once more to free herself. If it meant so much to him she wouldn't hold out against him any longer, but she didn't want it this way without tenderness, without love, without any answering desire on her part.

His hands were tearing at the buttons of her overcoat and she heard the soft wool cloth tear and the click of one of the buttons as it spun across the dashboard and hit the window before it fell to the floor.

She tried once more to capture his hands, to pull them away from her shoulders, but his fingers were digging into her soft flesh with so fierce a grip that she could not move them.

She cried out in pain and this time he seemed at last to hear her.

'Judith, please!' He was pleading with her now, no longer forcing her in that frightening, impersonal way. 'It's not my fault — I wanted to marry you and they wouldn't let us — I can't go on any more. It's not fair, Judy — other girls do. The chaps at work talk about it. You're the only one who won't. You just don't love me enough.'

All fear was gone now, but she was trembling violently. She'd never seen Rocky so desperate or so distressed. She loved him in this moment in a completely different way. Her longing was not that of a woman whose desire had been awakened to equal that of the man she loved. It was a much more maternal desire to offer comfort and solace — to ease his torment and bring him peace.

Rocky was right. They'd wanted to marry and Rocky had been willing to wait until she was his wife. He'd been prepared to do things the right way and their parents hadn't let them. It was their fault if she and Rocky were to flout their standards of convention now.

There would even be a vicarious revenge on those in authority over them, for all they'd made herself and Rocky suffer. Besides, what harm could it do? They wouldn't be hurting anybody and Rocky wanted her so much . . .

She felt another brief instant of fear and indecision, but she pushed it quickly from her mind. If Rocky wanted proof of her love, he should have it. She turned back to him and held out her arms, the faint smile on her face neither a look of resignation nor resolve, but a strange mixture of both.

In the end, Rocky had been gentle with her, but once it was all over he knew that there had been little pleasure or satisfaction in it for Judith. He felt ashamed of himself, and at the same time angry with her. He knew this was unreasonable and yet his subconscious mind told him that Judith had acquiesced from pity and that to take her in such a frame of mind was humiliating and distasteful.

He'd been with other girls before he'd met Judith, but they had been quite different. They had expected him to make love to them as a finale to an evening out. He knew he hadn't been the first with them, and wouldn't be the last, but because it was all taken as a matter of course, it never bothered him and had meant as little to him as to them.

But Judith was different. It was the first time for her, and somehow she'd made him feel guilty and ill at ease, although he had not forced her against her will. She'd let him know she was willing and he was furiously angry with her for making him feel now as if he'd raped her. It wasn't fair!

He sat silently staring into the darkness, carefully avoiding the white bewildered face of the girl at his side. He was smoking in quick, short puffs and he didn't really want a cigarette. He wound down the side window and flung the end into the darkness. His mind was a vortex of indecision. He wanted to go away from this place, back to the lights of the town, back home, and yet he knew he mustn't do this. He couldn't just leave her now without saying anything. She would be expecting him to tell her he loved her, to talk about their future, to make plans, but how could he? He didn't know if she would be willing to meet him again on the same terms, and if not, how could they get back to the innocent boy-and-girl meetings of the past? His instincts told him that in a relationship such as this there was no going back, but would

Judith be willing to go on? Was this the right time to talk to her about it? If only she didn't look so appallingly young and defenceless! If only she didn't have that trusting belief in him! What gave her the right to assume that he could judge what was best for both of them? He hadn't wanted to be made to feel that he was responsible for her. He'd wanted to be equal.

Perhaps his father was right, and he was still too immature to take on the responsibilities of a married man.

'You don't get anything for nothing in this life, son.' His father's words came back to him with shocking clarity. 'The day you get married you've got to be prepared to give up your freedom and I don't mean just your bachelor freedom, to come and go as you please, but your freedom to decide what *you* want, what you think best for *yourself*. You'll have to start thinking in terms of what's best for the family and what will make someone else happy. I know you better than you know yourself, Rocky. I don't think you've reached that point, yet. You want Judith, and because you can't have her any other way you think you ought to marry her. But it's not as simple as that. It's a pity Judith isn't the sort of girl who'll let you have your way with her without a wedding-ring on her finger. It's my belief you'd soon get her out of your system.'

He'd argued fiercely with his father. Perhaps the more so because he unconsciously recognized an element of truth in what he said. Now he wondered if his father was right. If he were truly and genuinely in love with Judith, would he at this moment be wishing himself far away from her?

'Judith, I'm sorry . . . '

He'd spoken impulsively, as a logical conclusion to his thoughts. But, naturally, she was not to know what had been passing through his mind. And she turned to him, love and relief shining in her eyes.

She'd been so alone these last few minutes, she'd been so afraid that she'd disappointed him, and in some way she couldn't understand, failed him. But because of his apology, she put down his silent withdrawal into himself as regret for his actions.

'It doesn't matter, darling. I'm glad. I feel now that we really belong to each other. I love you so very much, Rocky.'

With an effort he put his arms round her, and kissed her lightly on the lips. He tried to tell himself that he had no reason to feel ashamed. Judith had known perfectly well what he'd wanted from her, and she *could* have refused. If she had no regrets, why should he have any? All the same, it had been a mad thing to do; apart from anything else, he'd given no thought to the possible consequence. Suppose they were unlucky, and Judith started a baby . . . his mind shied quickly from the thought. There was enough to worry about without anticipating anything frightful like that.

'Look, Judith, I think we'd better not stay here. It's bitterly cold and I'll bet you didn't have much lunch, or any tea.

Let's go back into Yeovil and find somewhere decent to have a meal.'

She nodded, happy to fall in with anything Rocky wanted. She sensed that it would do them both good to get back into the world of other people. There would be plenty of time after supper for them to talk and plan and think about tomorrow.

But somehow there wasn't time, after all. Rocky had been fired with a sudden rush of energetic good spirits and had whisked her away to dance. His mood was so light-hearted and exhilarated, that he'd carried her away on a wave of frivolous gaiety. They left the dance at the last moment and Rocky only just had time to rush her home in the car before midnight; only a brief moment to kiss her good night and tell her that he would ring her next day.

Judith knew her father was still up, for the light shone under the drawing-room door into the darkened hall, and she guessed that he was waiting for her return. She heard his voice calling her, and in sudden inexplicable fear, she ran swiftly up the staircase into her bedroom and locked the door. She stood with her back against it, breathing deeply. Presently she heard his heavy tread on the stairs, but he walked past her doorway and along the passage to his own bedroom. She let out her breath and walked slowly over to the dressing-table, switching on the lamp. Then she sat down on the dressing-stool and stared at her reflection in the glass. Her cheeks were burning hot in contrast to the icy touch of her fingertips against them. There was a feverish sparkle in her eyes, but deep dark circles beneath them. Tired though she was, she knew she couldn't sleep. Rocky had swept her away on an inexplicable surge of light-hearted gaiety, but now that she was alone the memory of that first hour with him was groping its way back into her mind.

She stared closer at her face in the glass, convinced that this could not be the same Judith who stared back at her. Surely nothing could ever be quite the same again. She'd left girlhood behind her this evening, and now she was a woman, a woman more deeply in love than ever. Surely her face had changed! She could not see any difference, but would other people see it? Would her mother look across the breakfast-table at her in the morning, and somehow know?

She realized with surprise that she wouldn't really care if her mother did guess the truth. It would be quite wrong to feel ashamed of love, and hadn't she and Rocky so often agreed that sex was only a means of expressing love? She stood up, the soft curve of her mouth hardening to a thin line of determination. She wasn't going to let anybody make her regret what had happened. If Rocky wanted her again she would say 'yes'. No one was going to make her feel sorry for what they'd done.

But this momentary elation deserted her when at last she'd climbed into bed and turned out the light. Loneliness engulfed her, and try as she might she could not feel that what had passed between them had really brought Rocky closer to her. He'd been in such a strange mood all evening. If only he were here now, with his arms around her, and telling her that she need never feel alone again.

Quite suddenly she realized that for all the magnitude of her actions tonight, nothing that had transpired had in any way helped to bring their marriage nearer. The hopelessness of their position was unaltered. In fact, if her father knew what she'd done, he would be even further prejudiced against Rocky, unless . . .

She sat up in the darkness and the colour flooded into her cheeks as she recalled the scene with her father in the bedroom at Mrs. Baddock's. He'd believed then that she and Rocky were marrying because she was pregnant. He'd openly admitted that if this were so, he would give his consent. And Gavin — he'd probably not meant it seriously, but when she told him about it he'd said: 'That gives you the trump card, Judith.'

Suppose it happened now! It would be the solution to all their problems. Her father would never refuse to let Rocky marry her, if it were so.

She lay back on her pillow, her mind racing. Did she really want a child? It would be wrong to bring a baby into the world simply as a means of forcing her father's hand. She and Rocky must want it for itself, and they'd agreed many times that they didn't want children, at least not until they were properly grown up themselves. If she were having a baby she couldn't keep on her job, and that would mean they would have to try to live on Rocky's salary, and it wouldn't be easy. But surely, they could manage somehow. Strangely, now that it was a real possibility, she wasn't so averse to the idea of producing a family. It would be Rocky's baby, so how could she help loving it?

Lots of people thought it a good

thing to have babies when you were very young. They said it was more fun for the child to have young parents. Certainly, she thought, not without bitterness, she would show more understanding of her daughter when she was seventeen, and in love, than her parents had shown of her.

But would Rocky mind? Perhaps he wouldn't want to accept yet another responsibility, before he had even passed his apprenticeship.

She wished desperately that he were here now so that she could ask him what he would feel about it, and wondered if he, too, had been thinking about it. Some new-found instinct warned her not to speak of it unless he first broached the subject. He might worry and it would be pointless to worry him about something which might never happen.

She closed her eyes, realizing that she was incredibly tired. But sleep would not come. Try though she might to avoid it, she kept remembering those moments in Rocky's embrace. She wished desperately that her mother were the kind of woman she could confide in. She had nobody, really, with whom she'd ever been able to discuss the intimate side of life. Her mother scrupulously avoided any mention of 'the facts of life' and what little Judith knew she had picked up from a friend at school now living far away in Scarborough, and from books she had read, professing to explain to the uninitiated what married life was all about.

Was it because she and Rocky were not married that tonight's experience had been so meaningless? She had always supposed that to be loved in this way must completely transform a woman, and awaken in her feelings she had never experienced before. Some novels she had read spoke of their heroine swept to dizzy heights of ecstasy. She, herself, had felt only anxiety, fear that she would not be able to answer Rocky's need, and that she would displease him in some way.

Ultimately, she had felt only surprise that it was all so basic, awkward and uncomfortable.

She could not bring herself to admit that any part of Rocky's love-making had been distasteful to her. That would have seemed disloyalty, and in some way to belittle their love for each other. No doubt, like the books said, time was needed for people to adjust themselves and that if she and Rocky could be together often in that way, she would begin to feel some of the emotions instinct told her she ought to feel.

The thought only pushed sleep further away and brought her fresh anxiety. Would there be 'other times'? Would Rocky expect her to go on like this every time they met, and if so was this what she wanted? She felt terrified, as if she'd set a snowball rolling and was now powerless to stop the gathering avalanche. Rocky wouldn't force her into submission, but suppose he were hurt if she refused? He might even believe that she didn't love him as much as he loved her. She did, she did! It was just that this side of love didn't seem to mean the same to her as to him. Was there anything wrong with her? If only there were someone she could ask. She thought of her doctor, a white-haired man even older than her father, and no doubt very competent, but definitely not someone to whom she could go and say: 'Please explain things to me.' If only he were more like Gavin Pelham, sympathetic, understanding, a man one instinctively trusted . . .

Even in this exhausted frame of mind, she was still able to smile a little at her thoughts. Whatever would poor Gavin think if she were to force these kind of confidences on him? As her mother would say, it would be 'most improper'. All the same, Judith found herself wishing that Gavin were not her employer but a much older brother, someone to protect her and advise as well as comfort her. She fell asleep and it was Gavin, not Rocky, of whom she dreamed.

7

Gavin settled himself more comfortably on the deep, cushion-strewn divan, stretching his long legs towards the artificial log-fire. He realized with some amusement that there was no heat issuing from it to warm his feet. The high temperature of the room was due to the admirable central heating system installed in the extensive block of modern flats.

In a little while the heat would probably be too much for him, but for the time being it was very welcome after that long, cold train journey from Yeovil. As the train rattled along, he'd wished he had not decided to go to Town, but having made the effort to get away for the week-end, he was now going to enjoy himself.

Helen, it appeared from the note she'd left for him, might not be back till six. He glanced at his watch and saw that he still had an hour before he could expect her. Helen's idea of six, in any case, might well be seven or eight!

He felt for his pipe and then paused uncertainly before lighting it, not quite sure if she would want the perfume-laden atmosphere befouled! It must be a year since he'd last been in this place, but even if he'd forgotten the layout of the spacious flat, the smell of her perfume was all too well remembered. He thought, though not without amusement, that for once the advertisers were quite right when they claimed that a particular scent could attract a man. Whatever Helen used, it seemed exactly to match her personality — heady, exotic, sensuous. Even in her absence, he could feel her presence here in the room and knew himself vaguely disturbed by it.

When she telephoned on Friday and suggested he spend the week-end here, she told him quite frankly that her previous week-end arrangements had been cancelled and that she didn't fancy a Sunday alone in Town — if he could get up, she'd be delighted to see him.

His pride nearly brought him to the point of saying he really couldn't come after all, just to fill in the gap because of her changed plans. He was to be used to prevent her getting bored. In the end, he had accepted.

He wondered if Judith thought he was behaving crazily. He had told her twice to cancel all Saturday afternoon appointments and then on Saturday morning said that he would keep them. Finally, at twelve o'clock he made her cancel them again. No wonder she had looked at him with frank curiosity but he could hardly explain his indecision to *her*.

Judith. He stared into the bowl of his pipe. He knew that if he closed his eyes her image would come back to torment him. He tried to switch his thoughts back to Helen. But it wouldn't do. For the last three days he'd been unable to rid himself of Judith's childish little face, with its enormous bewildered blue eyes and hurt little mouth. Damn it, what right had she to rouse in him this furious protectiveness? She was nothing to him, nothing. Why should he care because she looked so tortured and unhappy? It wasn't as if he *loved* her. He was only sorry for her. It had to be pity, and not love. Otherwise why should he have chosen to spend this week-end with Helen? A man didn't rush into one woman's arms when he knew himself to be in love with another, unless it were to prove to himself he wasn't in love with either of them.

He got up restlessly and strode about the room, touching a picture, a magazine or a vase of flowers without seeing them. He shook his head once as if by doing so he could clear his thinking.

He was just sorry for Judith, that was all. A month ago she had meant no more to him than a particularly efficient and reliable secretary. Which proved it wasn't love. Clearly he'd been spending too much time alone . . . had been concentrating too much on his practice and not allowing himself sufficient relaxation. It was beginning to tell on him and this week-end with Helen . . . well, ten years without a woman in one's arms was a long, long while.

He stared up at a large framed photograph of Helen — one of her publicity prints, and a very good likeness. She looked tremendously alluring and exciting with bared, creamy shoulders offset by the silvery darkness of a fox fur slung casually across one arm. The sparkle of those ornaments on the sheath-tight dress had come out well in print and accentuated the beautiful shape of her body. Desire moved in him, basic and simple, and he longed suddenly for six o'clock and her return. She would have made plans. Helen was always planning. Possibly cocktails first, and then on somewhere smart to dine and dance.

He turned once more to the cocktail cabinet beyond the Hi-Fi. Her note had said: 'Help yourself to a drink,' and he needed one badly. He poured out a double whisky and took it across to the window, pulling aside the heavy mushroom-satin curtains and staring down into the street below. The shop windows opposite were ablaze with lights and had the Christmas displays, strangely exciting and gay. He remembered last Christmas which he had spent entirely alone nursing an old Alsatian through a bad bout of distemper. He'd planned to go to Rosemary's but the dog's owner had also been going away and with a selfishness which shocked Gavin had told him that if he couldn't take the dog in, he would have to be put to sleep.

But he'd stayed alone at the surgery and all for nothing — the dog had died anyway with only Gavin to mourn him through Boxing Day. By then it was too late to go to Rosemary's and, anyway, the mood to be gay had left him.

He supposed he'd go to his sister's this year. It was always best to be with children at Christmas and Rosemary had written already to say the kids were counting on his being there. He wondered what Judith would be doing. Would she have to go through the farce of sharing the goodwill of the season with her two elderly parents? Or would she be able to escape with young Rockingham and have fun? A kid of her age should be laughing and gay and happy — the way she'd looked that evening the boy had come to the surgery to take her out in his car. He wished he knew what had happened that evening to wipe all the joy from her eyes and bring back that unhappy expression to her face.

Her eyes, he thought, were her best features — large, beautifully shaped and in contrast to the almost white fairness of her hair, fringed with dark, black lashes. They were the most expressive eyes he'd ever looked into — utterly unlike Helen's, whose expressions were enigmatic and mysterious no matter what her mood, not unlike those of the boy Judith loved so much. He, too, had dark-brown eyes. Maybe all dark-eyed people were inscrutable, he thought now. There was something attractive as well as mysterious in the colour. At least, it was infinitely preferable to the grey of his own.

'Why, darling, how lovely of you to be here waiting for me!'

Helen swayed across the room towards him. He'd been so lost in thought, he'd never heard the sound of her key in the lock. He stood up quickly, and as she leaned towards him her deeply-carmined mouth touched his lips. Then she stood back looking at him quizzically.

'Why, Gavin, I do believe you're grown more handsome than ever. Or perhaps you just seem so in contrast to that dissipated oil magnate I've been lunching with. Look, darling, what he gave me.'

She flicked at the very expensive orchid pinned to her smart black suit.

'I'll wear it tonight, Gavin, for you!'

Despite himself, Gavin smiled. Helen

was always so frankly depraved, one couldn't stay cross with her for long. She had no morals, no scruples and would, had he asked her, have told him quite openly that she only lunched with the oil magnate because he was rich and influential, and not because she liked him. Helen lived in the wrong era, he told himself as he went across the room to pour her a drink. She would have made a wonderful courtesan, perhaps ending up as a royal mistress with tremendous power and wealth and a shocking reputation, which would have made her very happy indeed.

She took the drink from him and flung herself down on the divan beside him, looking provocative and amused as she teased him about his 'dull old job'. He watched and listened and occasion-ally paid her extravagant compliments because he knew she expected them and because most of his remarks were true, anyway. She was beautiful and becoming more desirable every moment.

He accepted his third drink and knew

that he was well on the way to getting tight. Well, what harm in it? He'd forgotten Judith, forgotten his work and was enjoying himself. That's why he'd come, wasn't it? And to be with Helen.

'Darling . . . ' She moved slowly and gracefully into his arms. 'You don't really want that drink, do you, my sweet? And nor do I? Let's put them down and have them later.'

Her voice was infinitely soft and caressing and her body beneath his hands pliant and alive. He hesitated only for a moment before he drew her close against him and the orchid crushed between them added its own scent to the warm, perfumed air.

★ ★ ★

Later that evening they sat at a secluded table in one of the rather smart clubs of which Helen was a member. He was amused to discover quite how many men Helen knew, and it was nearly always a male head that turned and nodded, and never a woman who came across to the table to say: 'Hi, Helen, what's doing?' If he'd ever had any romantic illusions about her, they were gone now for good. It surprised him that he had ever thought of asking Helen to marry him. If Helen married, it would be to one of her 'Oil Magnates'. He wouldn't be a bit surprised to see her then in the headlines as the fifth wife of some multi-millionaire.

Yet for all this blow to his sentimental ideal, he didn't dislike her. She'd reduced life to a simple code which was briefly to amuse and be amused — primarily to be amused. He was vaguely flattered by the certainty she hadn't found him boring. To be a bore was the one deadly sin in Helen's eyes. Her love-making had been skilled and experienced, and he knew that she found him attractive. Somehow, it seemed as if she had reduced everything to a dispassioned simplicity. Sex was just that, and no more. She didn't pretend to be in love with him or even expect him to be in love with her. It was enough for her that they suited one another, and like a sleek, satisfied cat she smiled contentedly across the champagne glasses. In the background, a small orchestra was playing one of the tunes from *Gigi*. He recalled seeing the film in Yeovil a couple of years ago, and how charmed he'd been by Leslie Caron. For some inexplicable reason, the young actress reminded him now of Judith. They were totally unalike to look at and he pondered the elusive link between them, so hard to define.

'Penny for them, my sweet.'

Helen's voice, amused rather than curious, broke in on his thoughts. But Gavin knew he couldn't talk to her about Judith Bryant. There could not be two women more utterly opposite, and an account of Judith's elopement would only arouse Helen's amusement.

'I was thinking we might dance,' he lied quickly, and led her on to the crowded floor.

She danced very close to him, her cheek against his, her movements as always wonderfully graceful. Gavin was out of practice but he'd always loved dancing and after a moment or two he found he no longer needed to concentrate on the beat. In any case, the limited space made it impossible to do much more than shuffle. He knew that presently he would go back with Helen to the flat, that they'd probably have more drinks and that he'd make love to her again. And tomorrow? A late rise, drinks, lunch somewhere smart, and then he'd have to be thinking about the train home.

Quite suddenly, he felt deflated and depressed. It was all quite pointless. He probably wouldn't see Helen again for months. Even if he were willing to make the long journey to Town again soon, he simply couldn't afford to lead this kind of life for more than a few days at a time, and then rarely. He wasn't fool enough to believe that Helen would consider a week-end in Yeovil. In any case, she was off to Scotland next week to spend Christmas and the New Year in Edinburgh. If she'd been in love with him, what a different complexion it would put on the future. But such a thought was ludicrous. If nothing else, this week-end with Helen had put things in their right perspective. There'd be no more romantic illusions about her. He could even feel a moment's contempt for himself that he should still want her physically. He knew that if she were to refuse him the hospitality of her flat tonight he'd be disappointed. But there seemed little likelihood that he'd be asked to leave. On the contrary, Helen seemed to like him better than she'd ever done before.

'*Darling!*' she was saying in that low, husky voice of hers. 'You even dance well, too! You really shouldn't hide your light under a bushel. *Still waters run deep* — that proverb suits you.'

Gavin shook his head.

'Don't glamorize me, Helen. I'm really a very dull chap and I know it.

There was a time — ' He broke off, abruptly, unwilling to tell her about his pre-war character for fear she would follow up with questions about his war-time experiences. He wasn't prepared to discuss them with anyone — they were better forgotten and put out of his own mind, too. All the same, that year as a prisoner had changed him — irrevocably, and he knew it. He'd vowed then, in that cold, dark, miserable coffin they called a cell, that if he ever got out of it, and home, he'd do something worth while with his life — give up the irresponsible search for fun and make his life useful.

Sometimes he'd despaired of ever getting home. Sometimes he was near to losing his sanity. But as the weeks of solitary confinement and near starvation became months, he managed to adapt himself to solitude and kept his mind occupied working out a future he might never have. It was then he'd decided to become a vet. He'd known there would be five years at college before he could qualify but he was still only eighteen — he could afford those years. When his father and mother had died in the war, some years earlier, in the bad raid on Coventry, they'd left enough money for him to finish at his public school and go on to Cambridge. But by the time he was eighteen, the Korean war was in full swing. He'd wanted to join up so he hadn't asked for deferment from National Service, as some of the other boys who were going to University had done. The thought that he could afford those five years in a veterinary college was one he clung to. There wouldn't be much over afterwards — with luck, enough to buy a small country practice. That's what he wanted — peace and quiet and a chance to live close to nature. Animals were so much nicer than people. No animal tortured another as he was being tortured just for the fun of it. Animals killed to eat or to defend themselves. They weren't sadists . . .

Rosemary, bless her, had understood

and given him a home until those years in college were over. Of course, it hadn't all been hard work and there'd been a number of girls he'd taken around, and Evelyn. Perhaps it was Evelyn's duplicity which had pushed him back into his cell again — making him despise the human race — or most of it. At least Helen was honest, even if she were governed entirely by material advantages. He supposed, wryly, that if he'd been rich, she might now be his wife! Would he have been happy? Would she have been faithful to him? Would Ascot, Henley, Hunt Balls, the South of France, yachting and ski-ing have satisfied him? Deep down inside he knew that he wanted something more from life than an endless search for pleasure. He'd resolved to do something worthwhile if he ever got free and his work now was wonderfully rewarding. To alleviate suffering in others — even if they were only dumb animals — helped to alleviate his own cynicism with the human race, and restore his bruised mind and heart.

'Well, am I going to hear about your past?' Helen was watching his face closely, trying to guess at his thoughts. That was one of the intriguing things about Gavin — one couldn't ever be sure what lay behind that curiously attractive, lean, tanned face. She'd believed he was madly in love with her — that any time she wanted, she had only to lift her little finger and he'd come. Which he'd done this week-end. But somehow, even in the most intimate moments of love-making, he had seemed to elude her — to remain completely himself. This elusiveness added greatly to his charm. It stirred in her completely feminine make-up a desire to conquer him — make him a slave like those other men in her life. Yet she knew she would despise him once he weakened, just as she despised the others.

She reached across the table to lay long, cool, white fingers over his brown hand, and smiled at him provocatively.

'Never mind, my sweet — I'm not going to probe. Let's have a last dance and then go back to my flat, shall we?'

Gavin was quite ready to leave. Helen's voice and eyes held out a promise. As he felt her graceful body slide into his arms and seem to merge with his own in one simple, sensuous movement, he didn't want to refuse. Lovely, exciting Helen — with her beautiful body made for a man's delight; and her cold, empty soul.

8

'You're sure you're not, cold, Judith? I'm afraid the heater's not any too effective. One of these days when I can afford it I shall have to swop this old shooting-brake for something more comfortable. Still, she is reliable otherwise, and that counts for a lot.'

Judith made yet another attempt to respond to Gavin's light-hearted conversation. He'd been so wonderfully kind and considerate that the least she could do would be to try and make this Christmas a happy one for him.

She was still a little astonished to find herself here with Gavin, driving down to Dorchester, where she would spend Christmas with Gavin's sister and brother-in-law, Rosemary and Philip Hughes. Their kindness in inviting a complete stranger to their home for what was, after all, a family festival, was clearly indicative of the type of people they were. Rosemary had written such a tactful letter to Judith's father, that even he had seen the wisdom of getting Judith away from home surroundings to be with younger people.

When Gavin had first invited her to join him at Cherry Tree Farm, Judith had refused at once. She was still hoping that somehow or other she and Rocky might be able to spend Christmas together. But their elopement seemed only to have increased their respective parents' disapproval of their attachment. Rocky knew only too well how unwelcome he would be in Judith's home, and was forced to admit that his father had flatly refused to invite Judith to Christmas lunch with them. He seemed to feel that he owed it to his father to give way on this occasion. His father had had quite a task to get Rocky reinstated in the firm, and on the whole had been very sporting about the whole unfortunate week Rocky had been away. There had been no endless recriminations, such as Judith had to endure. In fact, his parents had been pretty decent to him in every way. But they did not want Judith in their home.

It wasn't just the thought of leaving Rocky behind that dampened her spirits and made her so quiet and thoughtful. It was the now ever-present fear that she was going to have his child. She kept trying to tell herself that her fear was born of a guilty conscience. She believed Rocky felt guilty, too. Since the one occasion they had made love, Rocky had avoided physical contact of any kind, only kissing her briefly and hastily when it was time to leave her at her home.

She thought of the book she had obtained at the public library, hidden in her dressing-table drawer. It had not given her much information as to the symptoms she might expect, and those symptoms she did have, such as feeling of nausea and exhaustion, were not supposed to occur until much later on.

Gavin gave a brief glance at the white

outline of her profile and noticed the odd little habit she had acquired recently of twisting her fingers together and untwisting them over and over again, when she was lost in thought. He was beginning to feel gravely concerned about her.

He said, gently:

'You've been looking terribly tired, Judith. This holiday will do you good. Haven't you been sleeping well?'

His solicitude was suddenly more than her overstrung nerves could stand. She felt the hot tears sting her eyes and she bit her lip quickly as she fought to control herself.

'N-n-not t-too w-w-well!' she stuttered, hesitantly.

'You're not worrying about anything? Worry plays the devil with one's sleep routine.'

The urge to confide in someone, anyone, was proving too much for her. She felt that if she didn't talk to somebody soon, she might go out of her mind. Gavin was older, and no doubt

161

an experienced man of the world. Perhaps he wouldn't be too shocked, too disgusted with her.

Suddenly, she found herself telling him about that evening in the car with Rocky.

'You see,' she ended, 'it wasn't really so much that I wanted it, but I wanted to make things easier for Rocky. Now I can't help wondering if he despises me for giving in to him. Mother has spent most of my adult life telling me that a man loses his respect for a girl who gives way. And I'm afraid I may be going to have a baby.'

Gavin turned away from her, afraid lest she should see the swift rush of anger that caught hold of him as he spoke. For the second time, he began to feel some sympathy for Harold Bryant. Was young Rockingham really such a swine, or was he just a silly young fool caught up in a set of circumstances he couldn't control? Whichever it was, Gavin could cheerfully have wrung his neck.

He said, quietly but firmly:

'I'm not one of those people who believe that an action is wrong simply because it is unconventional. It has always seemed to me that it is the mood behind the action that really counts. Taken in reverse, a gift unwillingly given is worth nothing. Do you understand what I mean?'

She nodded mutely.

'You gave yourself to your Rocky because you loved him and wanted to make life easier for him. No one should blame you for that, Judith, although it was a very silly thing to do. As to the outcome — well, surely things aren't too desperate. Rocky *must* love you and you've told me once that your father would be most unlikely to withhold his consent to marriage in such circumstances. So don't worry about it.'

Even as he spoke these words, Gavin realized how inadequate they were. 'Don't worry!' As if any young girl could fail to be worried in such circumstances. He could understand only too well how desperate Judith must be. Desperate and shocked — just as he was shocked. It was all very well to hold modern ideas about sex and young people growing up to disregard the conventions. Somehow with a child like Judith, it was wrong — and nothing could make it seem right to him — or, no doubt, to her.

Wryly, Gavin recalled the week-end he had just spent with Helen. Certainly he was in no position to criticize Judith's or Rocky's behaviour. And yet it was different — Helen was an experienced woman of the world and knew exactly what she was doing and how to avoid suffering the consequences. Judith was a child — completely inno-cent — and Rocky had taken advantage of her love for him to gain his own ends.

The only comforting thought was that now her parents would certainly allow her to marry the boy. Yet even this thought failed to make Gavin feel easier about the situation. So often marriages made in order to give a child a name and protect the girl were doomed to failure. And with her romantic ideals, Judith could not want it this way — a hurried, hushed-up wedding.

He felt a fresh wave of pity for her — of dislike for the boy who had got her into this mess — and a longing to protect her.

But the relief of having told someone had helped Judith to review her position less despairingly. It might not be true. And if it were, Rocky would certainly marry her. True friends such as Gavin might not approve, but at least he did not despise her as she had feared he might. She resolved not to think about it any more than she could help and tried to evoke an interest in the people she was about to meet. Gavin was only too pleased to answer her questions about his young nieces and nephew, to whom he was obviously devoted.

The children were in bed but not yet asleep when they arrived at the lovely old Dorchester farmhouse just after seven o'clock. Almost before Rosemary had opened the front door to them, two small pyjama-clad figures were hurtling down the narrow, twisting staircase and they flung themselves upon Gavin with glad cries of welcome.

Gavin hugged them both and detached himself from their soft little fingers while he tried to introduce Judith to his sister. In the midst of the bustle and confusion, Judith had a quick impression of a friendly, motherly sort of face, utterly unlike Gavin's. But she felt sure she was going to like Rosemary. She accompanied her up the staircase and when the children were tucked up in bed and Rosemary was showing her into her room, her first impression was confirmed.

'I'm so happy you could come,' Rosemary Hughes was saying, as she turned back the candlewick bedspread. 'We live such a secluded life down here and we've often wished Gavin would bring some of his friends to see us. Now at last he's done so.'

There were Christmas roses on the

dressing-table, magazines and a *Reader's* Digest on the bedside table. There was even a log fire burning in the stone grate, which Rosemary now poked into a cheerful blaze.

'We so seldom use the spare room, I wanted it properly aired and warmed for you. It would be too awful if our one and only guest were to go home with rheumatism.'

She waved aside Judith's 'thank you's' and told her that she could have a hot bath before she changed, if she wished, since supper would not be ready for another half-hour.

'I'm so *relieved* the water's hot!' she prattled on, cheerfully. 'Phil promised he'd pull the damper out but with our antiquated old boiler you can never be sure.'

With a last friendly smile at the younger girl, she left Judith alone.

Judith stared round the lovely mellowed room, shining in the firelight, and with a tiny shiver recalled the cold box-like room at Mrs. Baddock's.

Rosemary was obviously immensely houseproud and domesticated and her simple, good taste showed in her choice of curtains and furniture. It was a lovely room, and already she felt at home in it.

'I'm glad I came!' she thought, with a further lift of her spirits. The two, rosy-faced, noisy children had looked enchanting, and Gavin had said that the eighteen-month-old baby, April, who must be asleep in her cot, was equally enchanting. It would be fun, seeing their excitement in the morning as they opened their presents; fun to be part of a real family Christmas. She'd never quite realized before how meaningless Christmasses had been at home, with only herself and her parents there.

Supper was a simple, informal meal. It was served in the large farmhouse kitchen, which was beautifully warmed by the old-fashioned range. Rosemary jokingly criticized it but she had managed to cook a delicious jugged hare in it which Philip had shot a week ago. Judith liked Philip Hughes almost as much as she liked Rosemary. He was a short, angular man with slightly greying hair and large horn-rimmed spectacles, but behind them his eyes twinkled with the same merriment and good humour as Rosemary's. A lot of the time they spent teasing each other, but in such a way that their devotion was always apparent. Judith could not help wondering if in years to come she and Rocky could become like these two, completely satisfied and content with one another, complementing one another, the two people together making one whole.

The meal over, the two men disappeared into the drawing-room for a game of chess. Rosemary was persuaded by Judith to let her help with the washing-up.

'I rather like washing-up, especially in a lovely warm kitchen like this. I envy you your home, Mrs. Hughes.'

'Please call me Rosemary, or I shall feel I've committed a *faux-pas* in calling you Judith. But Gavin always wrote of you as Judith, and not Miss Bryant.'

Judith was a little surprised to realize that Gavin had mentioned her in letters at all. She wondered just how much he had told his sister about her and Rocky, but Rosemary soon cleared up these doubts.

'Phil and I thought it such a shame that your father should have found you in Scotland before you'd been there long enough to get married,' she was saying as she plunged her square, capable hands into the bowl of hot, soapy water. 'I know you are both terribly young but young people are growing up much more quickly these days. Do tell me about your fiancé. Gavin says he's very good-looking.'

Again, Judith was surprised, for Gavin had never passed any comment after his one meeting with Rocky, and she often wondered what he thought of him. Warmed by Rosemary's friendly interest, she tried to bring Rocky's image into this room so that she could describe him accurately. But strangely, she could not place him here, and when she tried to list his good qualities she found herself saying, inadequately, such things as: 'He dances awfully well' and 'We always have such fun together.'

Her last remark was misleading, for Rosemary said:

'I always say a sense of humour is one of the most important ingredients in a marriage.'

It wasn't quite true that Rocky had a sense of humour. He was more often intense than light-hearted, and by 'fun' she had meant that they'd managed to have a good time together.

She turned the conversation away from Rocky to Rosemary's children. At once, like all mothers, Rosemary broke into a loving account of her three offsprings.

'Terry, the eldest — he's nearly six — always reminds me of Gavin when he was a small boy. Of course, I'm ten years older than Gavin, so we never suffered from the usual brother-and-sisterly squabbles. I suppose I was always rather maternal, even as a young girl, and Gavin seemed like my own child. Whenever I have to deal with Terry in an awkward mood, I'm reminded of the days when I had to cope with Gavin. In a way, it makes managing Terry quite easy for me.' She lifted some more dishes off the draining-board.

'Now Phyllis — she's a completely different kettle-of-fish. She's only four, but it's obvious she's going to be exactly like my Phil. You probably noticed she's tiny for her age, and dark-haired as Phil used to be before he went grey. I'm afraid Phyllis is going to need glasses, too. Then of course there's April. She's not like anybody unless it's a Botticelli angel, all gold curls and blue eyes . . . ' She gave Judith a quick look, and added: 'A bit as I imagine you must have looked, Judith. Gavin dotes on her, the little minx. Of course, he's frightfully fond of Terry and Phyllis and he spoils them all equally, but April has only got to crook her little finger at him and he comes running. It's really time Gavin got married and started a family of his own. He'd make a wonderful father, don't you think so, Judith?'

Judith had never really thought about it. Now that she did, she could appreciate that Rosemary's remarks were justified. She'd often noticed how wonderfully gentle his hands were when he tended the sick animals in the surgery. He seemed to instil trust and confidence, even while he was forced to hurt them. She could imagine those same long, gentle fingers soothing a fretful baby, and making it feel better just by his touch.

'Why *hasn't* Gavin married?' she asked, curiously.

Rosemary shrugged her plump shoulders and said:

'I suppose he has just not met the right girl. There was a girl once but she damn nearly broke his heart and it's a good thing I never met up with her afterwards. And then last summer he mentioned a model, a girl called Helen,

I think. But it didn't seem to come to anything. Phil and I were wondering about it. To tell you the truth, Judith, we'd been wondering about you, too. I suppose like all happily-married couples, Phil and I want everyone else to be happily married, too, and Gavin's only got to mention a girl for us to start hearing wedding bells. When he wrote in such glowing terms about your efficiency as a secretary and how well you managed the animals, we thought you sounded absolutely right for him!'

She laughed and then sighed.

'We were really quite disappointed when the letter came about you having gone off to Gretna Green with your Rocky. Anyway, I can see now that you're years younger than Gavin. We should have accused him of baby-snatching,' she ended teasingly.

They'd come to the end of the dishes and Rosemary collected the coffee tray, beckoning to Judith to follow her along the stone-flagged passage to the drawing-room.

A huge log fire blazed in the open hearth and the room looked warm and inviting. The two men were sitting a little to one side, so engrossed in their game that it wasn't until Rosemary put down the coffee tray with an extra clatter that they jumped to their feet apologetically.

Judith was delighted to see how charmingly Phil Hughes took care of his wife. Without appearing to fuss unduly, he seemed to anticipate her needs.

Gavin, too, had beautiful manners and Judith could not help contrasting his behaviour with Rocky's. It was not that Rocky had bad manners, but that his attitude to her was far more casual, more that of an equal than Gavin's. Where Rocky would throw her gloves to her, saying: 'Hi, catch!' with a cheerful grin, Gavin had carried them across the room and held them out to her, saying: 'You'll need these, Judith. It'll be a cold drive.'

As she sat in companionable silence with Rosemary in the drowsy heat of the log fire, she tried to puzzle out the reason for this difference in the two men. She decided that it was the ten years difference in their ages. Gavin seemed closer to a pre-war generation, whereas Rocky was essentially typical of her own age-group. Amongst the other young couples at the tennis club and at dances, Rocky's behaviour to her seemed perfectly normal. It was only when she was with people like Gavin and Phil Hughes that she was aware of a rather pleasant facet lacking in her contemporaries. There was something very satisfying in being treated as a member of the weaker sex — being made to feel protected and cared for.

Once or twice, Judith had found herself despising her mother's helplessness and the way in which she referred every decision to her husband, never seeming to have an opinion of her own. Judith had secretly resolved she would never let any man dominate her so completely and Rocky's treatment of her as an equal had flattered and pleased her. Now, curiously, she was no longer quite so sure what she wanted.

Without realizing it, she had been staring at the back of Gavin's head bent over the chess-board, and when he turned suddenly and smiled at her she was momentarily confused.

He stood up, saying to Phil:

'Let's finish this game tomorrow. I've so much to talk to Rosemary about.'

Phil acquiesced at once and soon they were joined in a friendly conversation from which Judith was not allowed to feel excluded. When at last she went up to bed she realized that these few hours with Gavin's family had done an enormous amount to restore her to her normal frame of mind. Gone was the desperate hopeless feeling that had clamped down on her for the last week. Although nothing really had been altered, just being with Gavin and the Hughes had given her a sense of security. It was almost as if she had been homeless and had now been adopted into a family who welcomed and cared about her.

For the first time in months, she fell asleep almost as soon as her head touched the pillow and the same light-heartedness stayed with her when she woke next morning to the sound of childish screams of delight outside her door.

Christmas morning! She jumped out of bed and ran to the window, pulling back the pretty, quilted chintz curtains. There was no snow, but a sparkling sun glittered on a hard, white frost, making lace on all the trees as they reached up their bare arms to a cloudless blue sky. Somewhere in the distance, church-bells were ringing and Judith knew a moment of intense happiness before the door burst open and Terry and little Phyllis tumbled into the room, their small hands clutching gaily-wrapped parcels.

'Happy Christmas, Auntie Judith!'

They pushed the parcels into her arms and waited expectantly for her to open them.

Laughing, she bent down and gave them each a quick kiss.

Without waiting to put on a dressing-gown, she knelt on the floor between them and undid the parcels. The little girl's present was only just recognizable as a handkerchief sachet. Judith was prevented from misjudging this gift by Phyllis's shrill little voice saying:

'It's a satchel for your hankies, Auntie Judith. I really was making it for Mummy but she said to give it to you as I could always make her another one.' She stared up into Judith's face from her short-sighted, dark brown eyes, a dreadful anxiety written there.

'You do need something to put your hankies in, don't you? They get all losted in a drawer on their own.'

Judith hugged the little girl, complimenting her on the beautiful stitching, the design, the choice of material, until at last Phyllis relaxed happily beside her. Terry's present was an ashtray he had made from clay.

'I suppose you do smoke, Auntie

Judith?' he asked, anxiously.

Judith thought quickly, and replied:

'As a matter of fact, I don't smoke, Terry. But your present is just what I've been needing for my dressing-table at home. I've nothing to put my hairpins and safetypins in and they get so untidy on my dressing-table. I've been wishing for ages that I had a pretty little bowl I could put them in.'

Terry beamed, and she suddenly understood why Rosemary had thought him so like Gavin. His eyes crinkled at the corners in exactly the same way as Gavin's when he was amused.

She was glad that she had remembered to bring presents for the children.

It was a lovely beginning to the day, and as she hurriedly dressed and went downstairs to join the others at family breakfast in the kitchen, she knew that if only Rocky were here to share everything with her, life would be quite perfect. After breakfast, the adults exchanged gifts and Judith was touched to receive a very attractive handbag from the Hughes and a beautiful Parker pen with her initials on from Gavin.

'Your ball-point pens always seem to run out at the wrong moment, Judith!' he excused his extravagance.

She wished she had something nicer for him than just a new engagement diary but he seemed very pleased with it, saying he'd always had to buy one for himself before.

Everyone helped with the washing-up, and not long afterwards the entire family set off in Gavin's shooting-brake for the village church. Rosemary had arranged for someone in the village to come and cook the Christmas lunch and mind little April, whom they left happily cooing in her play-pen.

The Christmas service with its traditional carols should have been uplifting, but kneeling in the church Judith could think only of Rocky and the wedding they had never had. It hadn't seemed to matter when they discussed their Gretna marriage that she would have to forgo the conventional white bridal gown and

all that went with a church wedding.
But now, she longed with a dull ache to
be walking down this same aisle on her
father's arm, with Rocky standing at
the steps of the beautifully-decorated
chancel.

'Oh, Rocky, Rocky!' her heart cried
out in unbearable loneliness. She
suddenly bowed her head and prayed,
as she had not done in years, that there
would be no child. She wanted so much
to be able to be married in a church,
like any other bride, and to feel that
God truly blessed their union. When
would this be — if ever? Surely her
father must relent in time.

She felt Terry's small, hot hand on
her arm and heard his whisper:

'It's time to go, Auntie Judith.'

A few moments later they were out in
the bright sunshine and the Hughes
were introducing her to various friends.
Rocky was forgotten until they reached
the farmhouse, to be told by the daily
woman that a young gentleman had
phoned from Yeovil to speak to Miss

Bryant. Judith's heart missed a beat. It could only be Rocky.

'Is he ringing again? Did he leave a number? Did he say I was to ring back?'

The questions rushed from her mouth before she could stop them.

When she was told there was no message, her disappointment was acute. Then Gavin said quietly, at her side:

'Why not ring him back? I presume he'll be having Christmas lunch with his family?'

She looked at him gratefully, and still in her overcoat, followed him through into the drawing-room where he pointed to the telephone. He left her alone, closing the door behind him as he went out tactfully, leaving her undisturbed.

Her hands and voice were trembling as she asked for Rocky's number. It seemed an age before the childish voice which she recognized as Betsy's asked excitedly who was calling.

'It's Judith, Betsy. Could I speak to Rocky, please?'

'Rocky, it's Judith for you,' she heard

Betsy shout across the room, and remembered that in Rocky's house the telephone was in the dining-room, where obviously the family were already foregathered. A moment later she heard Rocky's voice:

'Judith — darling — I tried to ring you earlier — Betsy, be quiet, I can't hear properly — Judith, can you hear me?'

She tried to answer him, but her throat was suddenly choked with tears. At last she managed to wish him a happy Christmas.

'What did you say? Betsy, put that down. Yes, I'm just coming, Mother.'

There was a moment's silence, and then he said:

'I'm terribly sorry, Judy. I'd hoped to speak to you while the family were all at church. Are you all right?'

'Yes, and Rocky — I love you very much.'

'The same goes for me, too!' She guessed his reply was guarded because of his family's presence in the room, and suddenly the conversation seemed pointless.

As if Fate meant to intervene, the line suddenly went dead and then the operator's impersonal voice told her that she'd been cut off.

'If you'll hold on, I'll have you re-connected.'

'No, no don't — thank you — I'd finished, anyway.'

She replaced the receiver and stood for a moment looking at it in silence. It had sounded as if the Rockingham family were having a gay time. She suddenly hated herself for wishing that Rocky hadn't sounded happy, too. Perhaps it was the phone which had given his voice that excited tone, and he was really missing her as much as she missed him. She tried to be glad for both their sakes that on this particular day they had somehow managed to join in the spirit of Christmas although they were apart.

Much later in the afternoon, when the beautifully-decorated Christmas tree had been stripped of its presents and the children were engrossed in their new toys, the telephone shrilled again, causing all the adults to look in Judith's direction.

'I'm not expecting a call, Judith,' Phil Hughes teased her. 'It must be your young man again.'

Judith stood up, the colour flaring into her cheeks, in a way that enchanted Gavin who was watching her. He thought how beautiful she looked with that glowing colour, and her eyes alight and sparkling with anticipation. How emotional this child was — so easily cast from happiness to despair, and as quickly roused again.

But this time, the call was for Gavin.

Gavin went to the phone. Somewhat surprised, he heard Helen's voice at the other end.

'Darling, a happy Christmas and a thousand congratulations. You must be thrilled to the core. You are a dark horse, Gavin, never to have mentioned your Uncle Basil before.'

'My uncle?'

For a moment or two, Gavin couldn't think who Helen was talking about. And then he remembered his father's only brother, Sir Basil Pelham. The last time he'd seen this particular relative he'd been about two years old! Sir Basil had then decided to settle in Kenya where he had coffee estates, and after the death of his parents, Gavin had completely lost touch with this member of the family.

He recalled that his uncle had married and that there were two sons, and remembered his own vague feeling of distress when he'd read in the papers some time ago that the elder son had been killed in some dreadful way during the Mau Mau trouble.

'You must be speaking of my Uncle Basil in Kenya,' he said, still puzzled by her phone call.

Helen's voice came clearly back to him.

'That's right, Gavin. I suppose you didn't hear the news at lunch-time. So perhaps I'd better tell you. Your uncle has just died. And you, my dear boy, are the new Baronet.'

Gavin suddenly laughed. No wonder Helen was so excited, believing that he had inherited a title! She was going to be dreadfully disappointed when she heard that there was a much closer heir. Obviously, she hadn't heard of — what was the boy's name? — Edward.

But it was his and not Helen's turn to be surprised when she replied:

'But, Gavin, he's dead, too. He'd been mauled by a lion when on safari and he's just died in hospital. It was the shock of hearing about it that killed your uncle. He was obviously devoted to his son. Anyway, there's no doubt who inherits. The one o'clock news said that 'Gavin Pelham, thirty-year-old veterinary surgeon with a practice in Somerset, would succeed to the title.' I'm terribly glad, Gavin, but I must say I'm a bit surprised. I thought a baronetcy just flickered out if there was no son to succeed.'

'This was one of the ancient ones created by some monarch — I think it was Charles I — way back,' Gavin replied. 'I seem to remember my grandfather, Sir Guy Pelham, explaining to me when I was a boy that in this case the title could go to *'heirs male whatsoever'*; in other words, next of kin. But as I knew my father's elder brother would inherit, and then my cousins, I took it for granted I would never be in the running. Anyway, thanks for letting me know, Helen. If it's true, no doubt I shall be hearing officially, later.'

Gavin couldn't pretend a grief for people who were virtually strangers to him, but he was nevertheless shocked.

He hoped Helen wouldn't think him rude for cutting any further conversation off so abruptly.

Rosemary was looking at him, anxiously.

'I don't suppose it's true,' he said, unbelievingly, 'but Helen's just informed me that they announced Uncle Basil's death on the one o'clock news. His younger

189

son died, too, which seems to make me a *Baronet*.'

Gavin seemed strangely unaffected by the news. And Judith suspected that he still did not quite believe it. With a sudden sense of shock she realized that, if the rumour were well-founded, Gavin would be rich and there would be no need for him to continue with his practice. He wouldn't need her any more, either, and the thought was strangely depressing.

As if in direct answer, Gavin said suddenly:

'Well, one thing's certain at least. I'm not giving up my work to go haring off to Kenya. I'm far too absorbed in it. So let's forget the whole thing. Come on, Rosemary, I'm dying for a cup of tea.'

9

When surgery ended on New Year's morning, there was still an hour before lunch-time. As Gavin and Judith cleared up after the last surgery patient, Gavin said with a smile:

'I haven't a single call this morning, thank heaven. To tell you the truth, I had a few too many drinks in the pub last night. How are you feeling?'

She put away a bundle of swabs, and tried to smile back at him.

'I'm all right. I saw the New Year in on the TV. Rocky couldn't take me to the dance because he had relations staying and they had a family party at home.'

Gavin glanced once more at his engagement diary — Judith's Christmas present to him — and closed it with a bang.

'I think what we both need is a

drink,' he said firmly. 'I'll take you to my favourite pub. We can get a meal there, too.'

'Only if you'll let me pay for my own lunch,' Judith said, stubbornly. They had had this argument once before, the day after they returned from Rosemary's. Gavin smiled.

'When *will* you remember that it's now quite definitely established that I'm Sir Gavin Pelham, Bart., and *rich*!' He emphasized each word with a grin, and went on: 'The letter I had from my solicitors this morning said that they'd had preliminary details of the Will. Apparently I can, quote, '*Confidently expect a very large legacy.*' It appears my Uncle Basil ended his days a very wealthy man.'

They both laughed, neither quite able to believe yet that Gavin was now a real Baronet, and not just an impecunious veterinary surgeon struggling to make ends meet.

Judith took off her overall and was about to collect her coat when the surgery bell rang with sudden, sharp insistence. Gavin sighed.

'I wish to goodness people would read surgery hours and stick to them. They're written clearly enough and yet someone always manages to turn up just after we've cleared away.'

Judith opened the door and saw a rather beautiful young woman standing in the cold January sunshine.

'I'm afraid surgery's finished . . . ' she began politely, and then broke off, seeing that the visitor had no animal with her.

The woman was scrutinizing her quite openly.

'You must be Judith Bryant!' she said, in a low, husky voice. 'Is Mr. Pelham in?'

By now Judith had recognized the woman as the one in the photograph on Gavin's desk, but how much more beautiful in person. No wonder Gavin was in love with her. She looked as if she'd stepped off a *Vogue* cover — exotic, chic, completely poised.

Judith pulled herself together and stood aside for Helen to come in.

'Why, Helen of all people!' she heard Gavin's warm welcome, and then quietly closed the door on them and tactfully retired to the waiting-room which she knew needed tidying up.

Helen, for all she was so much taller than Judith, and the fact that she wore three-inch high heels, still had to raise herself on tiptoe to plant a perfumed kiss on Gavin's cheek.

'Surprise, darling!' she said. 'And a very happy New Year.'

He pulled his own chair forward and handed her a cigarette, apologizing that he couldn't offer her a drink.

'A pretty little thing, your secretary. I can quite see how those great big, sad, blue eyes could appeal to your chivalrous instincts, Gavin.'

He sat astride Judith's chair at the desk, and leaning his arms on the back, eyed Helen's faintly-smiling face. He decided that she wasn't being catty — merely teasing him — and said:

'Poor little Judith has been going through a bad time lately and you are perfectly right, one can't help feeling protective. But you, Helen, of all people! What on earth's brought you here?'

But you, Helen, of all people! What on earth's brought you here?'

She shrugged her shoulders and blew out a cloud of smoke.

'I've been staying with an aunt in Bath — and you're not to laugh, Gavin; that's perfectly true.'

He laughed all the same. Helen was not the sort of person who had aunts in Bath.

'I thought I'd look you up on my way back to Town. I've nothing to do today and there's no work in Town until after the week-end, so I thought a little diversion might be fun.'

It wasn't strictly true, of course. There were other reasons for her wishing to see him. There'd been no further news in the papers about Gavin's uncle, and she was burning with curiosity to know if it was really true. Completely honest with herself, as always, she knew that if it were, this could make an enormous difference to *her*. Without money, Gavin was merely an attractive pastime. With money *and* a title, Gavin more than fulfilled all the qualifications she demanded of a husband.

She'd been a little piqued that he hadn't been in touch with her since that week-end in Town and had even cut her rather short when she telephoned him at his sister's. Not that she could blame him. In past months she'd frequently left letters of his unanswered, and not bothered to ring back when her maid said he had telephoned. She wished she'd kept in closer touch, under the circumstances, but then who would ever have believed that Gavin Pelham might become a Baronet?

Far too clever to broach this subject at once, she said, lightly:

'Aren't you going to take me out to lunch, darling, now that I'm here?'

Gavin suddenly remembered Judith and said:

'I've just invited my secretary.'

Helen raised her eyebrows.

'A-ha! So we're mixing business with pleasure now! Well . . . I'm sure Judith wouldn't mind if you postponed the invitation to another day, would she?'

Gavin shook his head. He knew only too well that Judith lived for her moments with Rockingham, and that he, Gavin, meant practically nothing to her except perhaps a kindly confidant.

He made his excuses to Judith and let Helen drive him in her smart little scarlet sports car, not to the pub where he would have taken Judith but to the smartest hotel Yeovil could offer.

Helen somehow managed to make the place look shabby. He marvelled at her elegance, at the beautiful, proud carriage of her head and the graceful way she walked.

There were quite a few people drinking in the American bar and many male heads were turned admiringly as they walked in. Other women, too, were noting Helen's ocelot coat and matching Cossack hat. As they perched on bar stools, Helen let her coat slip from her shoulders. Although Gavin did not know the material was jersey, he admired the simplicity of the smart little suit beneath, which seemed to mould itself round her slim figure.

He ordered Martinis, which he knew she liked. Helen reached for her glass and clinked it briefly against his own.

'To you, darling, and congratulations.'

He looked at her, puzzled.

'On your new title!' she explained casually. 'I suppose it wasn't a false rumour?'

Gavin laughed.

'I can't get used to it,' he said. 'It's true all right. Still, I don't suppose it will change anything in the long run, except that I shan't have to go prematurely grey worrying over unpaid bills.'

Her training as a model had enabled Helen to adopt any mask she chose, and her face gave no indication of the little thrill of satisfaction his words gave her.

'But, darling, it's bound to make some difference. After all, if you're going to be rich, you won't want to spend the rest of your life messing about with animals.'

'But I like 'messing about with animals', as you put it,' he told her, smiling. 'I'd be bored stiff if I didn't have some work to do, and quite frankly it's the only thing I'm trained for.'

This time, Helen could not prevent the tiny frown creasing her forehead.

'You can't be serious, Gavin? I mean, it would be quite mad to bury yourself in a place like Yeovil, when you don't have to.'

'Well, Yeovil's as good a place as anywhere else,' Gavin argued. 'I certainly wouldn't want a London practice, and since it has to be the country, there's a lot to be said for Somerset. You know, 'Green Hills of Somerset',' and he hummed the tune of the song that used to be a favourite of tenors at musical soirées.

199

She decided not to press this point for the moment. She felt sure that in time Gavin would think differently. He must have some idea of the doors that would be open to him in the future and she couldn't believe that a person existed who wouldn't want the money'd way of life that wealth could bring.

'I'm afraid I'm rather a dull old stick,' Gavin apologized.

'That isn't how I would describe you, Gavin,' Helen said, looking at him provocatively. 'Remember the wonderful weekend we had in Town?'

He hadn't forgotten. He was a little surprised to know that it had meant more than just a little bit of fun to Helen. Breaking her journey back to Town just in order to see him was so foreign to her normal behaviour towards him that he was partly flattered, and partly embarrassed. He suspected she wanted to repeat the episode. And if she did? He wasn't at all sure how he would feel. Something curiously old-fashioned in his make-up vied with the baser male instinct to take advantage of a situation such as this. A love affair which was purely a gratification of the senses was not what he really wanted from life. He wanted to be like other people, to fall in love and be loved, to raise a family and build a home.

Almost as if she read his thoughts, Helen touched his sleeve where a button was missing, and said:

'You know, you really ought to get married, Gavin. You need someone to look after you.'

Gavin grinned.

'It's really not as bad as all that, Helen. My 'daily' does my mending, but as I wear this same jacket for work nearly every day, the poor woman hasn't had a chance to sew on the button. Anyway, I've lost it.'

But he was surprised and touched that she should have noticed such a detail. Something, or someone, was changing Helen. He noticed it again while they were at lunch. Her voice was somehow gentler, and if the adjective did not seem so absurd in relation to Helen, she was almost tender towards him.

'I presume your 'daily' doesn't 'live in'?' she questioned him. 'Since I don't have to hurry back to Town, would it shock the neighbourhood if I stayed the night? I probably could, if you wanted me to.'

Gavin had a quick mental picture of his rather shabby little house, contrasting with his vivid memory of Helen's flat. Somehow, he didn't think his place would appeal to her, and certainly he couldn't see Helen against such a setting. No central heating, a rather hard uncomfortable sofa in the box-like sitting-room, and an equally hard single oak bed upstairs. Besides, Mrs. Dawson would be in at eight o'clock to cook his breakfast the following morning.

Helen did not argue the point, but suggested that since she couldn't stay with him, he might like to drive her back to Town and stay at the flat. If he was busy this afternoon, she wouldn't mind a bit waiting here until he'd finished his rounds, or whatever he did. Again, Gavin refused. Friday was market day and often the busiest of the week. After the Christmas holiday it would be likely to be worse than ever.

Helen was peeved, but took good care not to show it. She knew better than to be too obviously chasing a man. It was always best to let him do the running.

Gavin was glancing at his watch now, and saying awkwardly:

'I shall have to push off in a moment, Helen. Much as I hate the thought of leaving you, I promised a farmer I'd have a look at one of his calves, and as he's one of my best clients I really can't break the appointment.'

Helen stood up and said, sweetly:

'Then I'll drive you back to the surgery, darling. It's been a lovely lunch, and I'm so glad I stopped off. Let me know when you have a few spare days.'

Outside the surgery, Gavin said good-bye, kissing her lightly on the cheek. He removed himself from the luxurious interior of her car and climbed into his shooting-brake. Helen watched him disappear round the end of the road, in a cloud of smoke from the exhaust. But instead of restarting her engine, she got out of the car and rang the surgery bell. She was in no hurry to get back to Town and a little talk with Gavin's secretary might result in a few more details about Gavin she wished to have.

'I think I must have left my gloves in Gavin's room,' she told Judith as an excuse for her return. 'Perhaps I could have a look?'

Her half-hearted search of course proved fruitless and she turned to Judith with a charming smile.

'I expect you love your work here,' she said in a friendly way. 'It must be very interesting.'

Judith looked at the older woman admiringly. How wonderful to have that poise, that wonderful way of wearing clothes. If she could only look like that, how much more Rocky would love her.

Her father, too, might think twice about the way he treated her. One couldn't imagine anyone dictating to Helen how she should run her life.

'Yes, the work is interesting,' she said warmly. 'And Gavin — Mr. Pelham — is a wonderful person to work for, and so kind.'

Helen had noticed the use of Gavin's Christian name, and just for a moment was touched by a faint tinge of anxiety. Was it possible that Gavin felt more than pity for this pretty child? He was just the sort of person to be bowled over by the young and helpless. If anything went wrong between Judith and her boy-friend, she could well envisage that Gavin would take on the role of confidant and comforter, which could be dangerous — very dangerous.

'Gavin tells me you're going to be married soon.'

She saw the colour rush to Judith's cheeks.

'Well, we're not even officially engaged yet . . . we're both rather young and our parents think we should wait.'

Helen was at once warmly sympathetic.

'But that's too old-fashioned for words. I believe young marriages are by far the best. It may mean a financial struggle in the first years, but in my opinion that draws couples much closer together.'

The lie slipped easily from her lips, for Helen was a great believer in the adage:

'*When poverty flies in through the window*
Love flies out at the door.'

Judith was looking at her with enthusiasm.

'That's just what I think, Miss Rowe. Besides, I should be able to go on working for Gavin and so we would both have our salaries to live on. We shouldn't be *really* poor.'

Helen put a friendly hand on the younger girl's arm.

'Then why don't you take the law

into your own hands, and just get married?'

Somehow, it no longer seemed strange to Judith that she should be discussing her private life with Gavin's friend. Helen Rowe was so charming, and so obviously interested. Helen inferred that now Gavin had come into some money, they would be getting married soon. It was nice to think they could be friends.

She found herself telling Helen about the elopement to Scotland and how since their return Rocky's attitude seemed to have changed. It was due, she was sure, to his father's influence. She did not of course tell her that she was afraid she might be having Rocky's baby.

Helen summed up the situation. From the sound of it, the boy was weak. If Judith wanted to keep him, she would have to counteract his father's influence.

Choosing her words with care, she led Judith to believe that she'd been handling Rocky quite the wrong way.

Rocky, she said, was the type who needed someone to make up his mind for him. Judith should help Rocky to stand up to his father.

Her words put Judith into a state partly of excitement, and partly of fear. Helen made it sound so easy and yet at the back of her mind she remembered Rocky's words, the last time they discussed the future. *'I think it would be more sensible to wait a few years. I ought to finish my apprenticeship and pass my exams . . .'* Was this really Rocky's true belief, or just an attitude his father had forced on him?

Seeing her hesitation, Helen said, lightly:

'Nothing in life can be achieved without a little courage, Judith. And if you and your boy should decide to elope again, come to my flat in London and I'll do all I can to help you.'

'How kind you are!' Judith said, impulsively, little realizing that Helen's only interest in her and Rocky was to remove her from Gavin's orbit.

10

Since Judith returned from her Christmas holiday she looked so very much better that her parents remarked on the change in her.

Judith was going out with Rocky and she was happy and excited. She hadn't seen him since she'd been to Dorchester for Christmas and the thought that in a few hours he would be calling for her had brought a happy glow to her face and eyes. Not even the depressing fear that she might be having a baby could outweigh her feelings of well-being. But her face darkened at once when her father remarked:

'The moment you get away from that boy you become a different person, doesn't she, Olive?'

Childishly, Judith flung back at him:

'It might be truer to say that I'm looking better because I've been away from this house. All you and Mummy can do is to run Rocky down. You're bigoted and prejudiced and I can't stand much more of it.'

Harold Bryant had always disliked being thwarted. Although some inner part of him admired Judith, even as a little girl, for standing up to him, he never failed to be stung when she did so.

'That's quite enough of that, my girl,' he said, banging the table with his newspaper. 'If you can't mend your manners a bit, I shall forbid you to go out with Rockingham tonight.'

Judith flung back her head, her cheeks red now with temper instead of happiness.

'You talk as if I were a child, Father. Short of locking me in my bedroom, which would be too stupidly Victorian for words — you can't stop me going out. I'm warning you, if you break your promise to let me go on seeing Rocky, I shall run away again.'

Her mother raised a protesting hand, and said weakly:

'Now, now, Judith, that sort of talk will only make your father angry. You know very well that is hardly the way to elicit his help.'

Judith swung round on her mother, exasperated.

'Perhaps you can tell me the right way, then. I've begged, cajoled, pleaded, done everything I can think of, to make Father understand that Rocky and I want to be married. I might as well talk to a brick wall. As far as I can see, he doesn't intend to give his consent now, or later, or ever.'

Harold Bryant looked at his daughter coldly. He disliked intensely such family rows and more particularly at breakfast. There seemed to have been no peace in this house ever since Judith had met young Rockingham.

'The way I feel at the moment, Judith, you're probably quite right.'

He hadn't meant to speak so openly or arrogantly, and he was a little shocked to see the colour drain from Judith's face and to see the trapped, despairing expression in her eyes. For a moment she looked beaten and then slowly her mouth tightened, her shoulders straightened, and looking straight at him she said:

'After what's happened, you may be *forced* to give your consent.'

Then she swung round on her heel and hurried out of the room, closing the door firmly behind her. Her parents looked at each other in shocked silence. Mrs. Bryant said, nervously:

'Oh, I'm sure she didn't mean *that*, Harold. Judith wouldn't — I mean she couldn't . . . I mean — ' She broke off, unable to discuss frankly such matters with her husband.

Harold Bryant, however, had no such reticences.

'If that boy's got my daughter into trouble, then by God, I'll horsewhip him with my own hands. I believe she meant it, Olive. That young whippersnapper must have planned the whole thing. I'll bet he's done this deliberately, to force my hand. Don't you see the game they're playing? They both know damn well a man in my position can't have an illegitimate child in the family — '

He broke off, pushing his chair back clumsily, and knocking over his cup of coffee without heeding the mess or his wife's restraining hand. He marched across the room and lifted the telephone.

While he waited to get through to Thomas Rockingham, he went on muttering to himself.

'I'll get to the bottom of this. We'll see what the young man's father has to say.'

Rocky's father was about to leave for work when the phone rang and, none too pleased to be held up by a caller at the last minute, he lifted the receiver.

'Oh, Bryant! What can I do for you?'

'I want to know what your son has been up to with my daughter,' Bryant's voice raged back at him over the wires. 'I'm telling you, Rockingham, if there's anything in this I'll have your boy flung out of the town.'

'What has Rocky done?'

Bryant's reply came back, shocking him with its brevity.

'I think my daughter is pregnant by your son.'

Thomas Rockingham drew in his breath sharply. His first instinct was to deny it and yet, on reflection, he was none too sure. Rocky had been behaving a big oddly, lately. He'd been surly and, at the same time, unusually deferential to his father's wishes. Only the night before, they'd had a long talk about Rocky's future, and the boy seemed to have regained his earlier enthusiasm for his career. Suppose Rocky had made the best of those two days in Scotland — if one could call it 'the best', he thought wryly. If so, he couldn't altogether blame the boy. From what Rocky had told him, the pair of them had actually shared a bedroom the first night. The boy wasn't made of stone. But if the girl was in the family way, it would be the damnedest bad luck.

Hedging, he asked:

'Have you got any foundation for your suspicion, Bryant?'

'I've had it from Judith's own lips.'

'Well, that's a bad state of affairs,' Rockingham said inadequately. 'But it's no good you blowing your top at me, Mr. Bryant. It's not my fault. If your daughter chooses to misbehave herself with my boy, she'll just have to take the consequences.'

Harold Bryant gasped.

'It's up to you, Rockingham, to see your son faces up to his responsibilities. If not, I'll have him branded publicly for seducing my daughter. He's not going to get off scot-free while my Judith suffers.'

Although inwardly he was as perturbed as was Judith's father at the news he'd been given, Thomas Rockingham was too proud a man to take kindly to this hectoring criticism of his lad. Craftily, he said:

'I don't think you're likely to do that, Bryant. I don't imagine a man in your position will want it made public that his daughter's having a baby. I'll see the girl gets proper financial compensation and maintenance for the child, but I'm not going to have my boy forced into a marriage that can only do him harm. Be reasonable, Bryant. A week or two back you were as anxious as I to put an end to this association and stop them marrying one another. I think my boy's begun to realize that he isn't ready for marriage and it must be obvious to you that he can't afford a wife, far less a child before he's even finished an apprenticeship. I've had some long talks with my boy since he's come home, and it's my belief he has begun to see sense. Fortunately, he's still a minor and I'll state categorically, here and now, that while I have control over him I'm not going to have him forced into a marriage he doesn't really want.'

And with that he slammed down the receiver, and was about to walk out of the room when he collided with Rocky.

'Aren't you coming, Dad? We're

going to be late.'

The older man looked at his son angrily.

'You young fool! Surely you know better than to play fast-and-loose with a girl like Judith Bryant. I can't think why you young people nowadays can't have more control — and some common-sense.'

Rocky raised his eyebrows, completely nonplussed. Thomas Rockingham felt his anger cooling and a little of the common sense he'd recommended to his son came to the forefront of his mind. This whole affair wanted careful handling. He didn't want the boy rushing off in an agony of remorse and marrying the girl just to make an honest woman of her. To antagonize Rocky now would be the very thing to make the boy act emotionally rather than logically.

'Now see here, Rocky,' he said more gently, 'I've just had Harold Bryant on the phone. It appears that Judith might be going to have a baby.'

He noted Rocky's white, shocked

face, not without pity.

'It's bad luck, but if it's true, there's not a great deal we can do about it.'

'But it can't be true, it *can't*!' Rocky protested, and then realized that it very well could. His first feeling was one of dismay at the unfairness of a fate which could punish him for one moment of weakness, and it *had* been only one moment. He'd never asked her again and he'd done his best to forget about it. It was damn bad luck. And then he thought of Judith, and what a terrible thing this was going to be for her. He and Judith would have to get married as soon as possible. Her father would be sure to give his consent now.

The older man laid a restraining hand on Rocky's arm.

'There is to be no repetition of the Gretna Green episode, Rocky,' he said firmly. 'I'm not having you forced into a marriage that wouldn't be right, just because of this mistake.'

Rocky stared at his father, shocked into protest.

'But, Father, what else can I do? It'll be my child . . . I owe it to Judith — '

'You don't owe her anything, boy,' his father interrupted. 'What you did was with her consent and you're both equally responsible. It's always harder on the girl in these cases, but nowadays there's plenty can be done for 'em. She could have the child adopted, for instance.'

Without being aware of it, they both walked out of the house and from force of habit had climbed into the Hillman and were driving towards the factory on the outskirts of the town. Rocky watched the cars passing them, without really seeing them. Surely his father, whom he'd never known do an unkind act, couldn't be serious about Judith. Of course he must marry her. Apart from it being his duty, he *wanted* to marry her. This was what he and Judith had been fighting for, for so long.

He was suddenly quite frighteningly unsure of himself. Did he really want the responsibilities of marriage? He certainly didn't want a child. Hadn't there been a vague feeling of relief when the Gretna Green episode had fallen through? Hadn't he settled down again to home life and his studies, almost as if there'd never been anything to interrupt them?

'But I do love her, I *do*!' he told himself, wildly. He thought of her small, oval face, and those large trusting blue eyes, and forced himself to remember the touch of her soft young body in his arms. But all feeling of desire for her was gone. He could feel only a terrible concern, a sense of guilt, and perhaps, most of all, a feeling of pity. He couldn't let her down. He wouldn't be able to stand the look in her eyes, or to live with himself with the thought of her facing disgrace alone. She had nobody, really; only that pompous Victorian father and that silly fluttering mother. The few friends she'd had when he first knew her, she'd dropped completely so that she could spend all her free time with him. He was only just beginning to realize how complete and absolute was her devotion, and what a stranglehold such devotion could be.

The sight of his father's square, familiar frame in the driving seat was suddenly comforting. How lucky he was to have someone to turn to, to advise him. In recent years, he'd so often resented his father's authority and longed for freedom from it. But now he was glad to be able to turn to his father and say:

'Well, what *am* I going to do, Dad?'

'Nothing, Rocky. Absolutely nothing.'

'But I'm seeing Judith tonight. I'm taking her to the cinema.'

'Then you'll have every opportunity to find out if the situation is as serious as we think. If it is, then I think you should be absolutely honest with the girl. You can tell her, if you like, that I've forbidden you to marry her. And, furthermore, that I've forbidden you to see her again. A complete break would be the best thing for both of you.'

'But I can't do that, Dad. For one

thing, I couldn't put it so bluntly; and for another, I want to go on seeing her.'

He was unprepared for his father's sudden burst of anger.

'You can put it any way you please, Rocky. Soften the blow as best you can, but deliver it all the same. And remember, I'm no longer concerned with what *you* want. I'm thinking now of what is best for both of you.'

'But I'm in love with her. You don't know what you're saying, Father. I couldn't just walk out on her even if I wanted to, and I don't. Besides, it's my child.'

The older man tried to gauge the extent of conviction which lay behind Rocky's outburst. Somehow, he'd never been convinced that Rocky was as much in love as he imagined. Judith was the first girl he'd ever taken seriously and maybe the boy did love her, after a fashion. But even this last declaration of love for the girl did not strike him as being completely whole-hearted. He sensed a hesitation and believed that if Rocky could only get out of this honourably, he was ready to do so. Of course, if the boy had really fallen in love, his obsession for Judith might last; but Thomas Rockingham doubted if Rocky was sufficiently mature to know the real meaning of the word 'love'; far less to experience it. It was different for Judith. Girls matured more quickly and he was quite prepared to accept as a fact that Judith was genuinely in love with Rocky. But there would be little happiness for either of them unless Rocky was capable of returning her love in full measure, even if there were no such complication as a child to handicap the start of their life together. It was quite impossible to visualize Rocky as a father — he was still only a boy, despite his height and manly appearance.

Thomas Rockingham was not an unkind man, and being a genuinely devoted parent he was acting as best he could in Rocky's interests. He knew it might be hard on Judith, but to break off this affair would ultimately be in her interests, too. But he decided not to try to press Rocky too far just yet. Most things were better done if they were done slowly, and the right word here and there would be much more effective than a too obvious laying down of the law. Indeed, he would not have felt very proud of his son if he'd given up the fight without a struggle. They would do their duty by Judith financially, and Rocky should be made legally responsible for the child's maintenance. It wouldn't do the boy any harm to have to pay for his misdeeds. Remembering Judith's pretty young face, he rather doubted that she would remain unmarried for long. Then Rocky would be free of her, and of the child.

By now they'd arrived at the factory, which put an end to the conversation.

His father brought up the subject of Judith again after tea. His manner was friendly and sympathetic.

'Don't think I don't understand what

a bad time you're going through, my boy. The fact of the matter is, you've got yourself in rather a mess, and what we've got to decide is how to get you out of it. Now don't think I don't admire you for wanting to do what you believe to be right for the girl. When you told me this morning that you intended to marry her, I know you meant it. But what you must stop to consider is whether a marriage in *these* circumstances is what is best for her.'

Rocky accepted a cigarette from the packet his father held out to him. He felt strangely close to him, the way he had felt in the days when Dad had kicked a football round the yard with him, and taken him fishing, and taught him how to hold a cricket bat. Their relationship was different now, no longer that of father and son. His father was speaking to him as an equal, and Rocky wanted to match up to this new status he had acquired in his father's eyes. He listened attentively.

'You see, boy, you don't know as

much about life yet as I do. You and Judith are not the first couple who have had to face up to this situation. In my day, a boy was expected to marry a girl if he got her into trouble, and there was no alternative. Nowadays, people think differently. Doctors and welfare officers, and the like, are all against what we used to call 'shot-gun weddings'. You and Judith have got to be absolutely sure you both love each other, and will go on loving each other, for the next fifty years.'

Rocky grimaced.

'That's absurd, Dad. Everyone knows marriage is a hit-and-miss affair. If it weren't, there wouldn't be all those thousands of divorces. How *could* anyone be sure? Judith might change, or I might change. You can't know what sort of person you'll be years from now.'

His father leant forward, eagerly:

'That's just my point, Rocky, and you've made it for me. People do change and the younger you are, the more chance there is of you changing as you grow older. D'you remember the first girl you ever thought yourself in love with? I'll bet when you think of her now, you thank your lucky stars you never went further than a kiss.'

Rocky looked at his father in surprise. Funny how often he'd thought of him as old-fashioned, and lacking in understanding of his generation. Yet what he was saying now was all too true.

'But, Judith . . . ' he paused, ' . . . I think it would break her heart.'

His father nodded.

'I'm not saying a break would be easy for either of you. Very often the right thing to do turns out to be the hardest. You know, son, you sometimes have to be cruel to be kind.'

'I don't see why we should stop seeing each other,' Rocky argued. 'I still love her, Dad, even if I'm not so sure now I want to get married.'

'Judith is young, Rocky, and with you out of the way it wouldn't be long before she'd find herself another man.

Of course,' he added quickly, 'she won't feel the same about him as she does about you, but with luck it'll be someone who's better able to support her, *and the child*, if it should come to that. The sooner you break with her, the sooner she's likely to find him.'

'I can't. I just can't, Father!'

The older man heard the lack of conviction that lay behind the words. The boy was still half in love, but no longer so sure of himself or his feelings. Well, he could make it easy for him. Better a few tears now than two, perhaps three, young lives completely ruined.

'Your mother and I were talking last night, thinking this house was a bit on the small side for us. Your mother said she'd never liked this street anyway, and now they're building that new estate — well, it mightn't be a bad thing if we up'd and moved to the other side of Yeovil. We could cut half-an-hour off our daily run to the factory.'

'What, move from here?' Rocky said,

incredulously. 'But we've been here twenty years . . . ever since I was born.'

'Oh, it'll probably be a wrench in some ways, but it's never a bad idea to make a fresh start, and since your mother is quite keen on the idea, it would seem to be the best answer to a lot of our problems. You and Judith wouldn't be on each other's doorsteps.'

'It would be a bit like running away . . . '

'Nonsense!' his father said loudly. 'You let Judith know it's all off and I'll talk to your mother and fix up the move. I give you my word, Rocky, I'll see the girl is properly compensated if there is a baby. If her father won't accept my money, I'll put it in the bank in Judith's name and then whatever happens, she'll be independent.'

Dad's being very generous, Rocky thought. It's not every father who would help the way he's trying to. He must be absolutely sure it's right. Dad's never put his money down unless it was a dead cert.

Rocky wondered if he would be able to make Judith understand that although he still loved her, it might be better to stop going around together. He realized with a sudden stab of shame that he didn't love her enough to face up to the possibility of fatherhood.

Nothing seemed to make much sense any more. He'd loved Judith enough to want to marry her when they'd eloped. Until then, he'd *known* he wanted to marry her. Judith hadn't changed, so why had he? The feeling he had now was rather like the morning after the only night he'd got really tight. It had been fun at the time, but the next day it had seemed stupid and rather disgusting. There was that other time, too, when he'd made love to Judith; at the moment of doing so it seemed the only important thing in the whole world. A while later he regretted it bitterly. Was he always to feel sick and ashamed after every impulsive action in his life? He'd understand himself better if he could only feel the same emotion from day to day. The last time they had gone out together he'd had a wonderful time with Judith. They'd recaptured the old, light-hearted gaiety and when he'd taken her home they had sat for a long while in the car, he making love to her wildly and passionately, though taking care of course not to lose his self-control a second time. How could he be contemplating, quite coolly, the thought of a complete break? It just didn't make sense. Maybe when he saw her this evening, he'd know for sure, one way or another, how he felt about her.

Weakly, he decided to leave a decision until then.

★ ★ ★

As evening approached, Rocky wondered, uneasily, what kind of reception he would receive at Judith's house. He expected her father would be waiting for him and dreaded the thought of the scene that must inevitably follow. He wondered if Judith would be watching for him from her bedroom window and would somehow manage to slip out of the house so that he needn't ring the doorbell and go in. Perhaps if he revved the engine up noisily she'd hear the car and come running out.

Deep down, he despised himself for this dread of meeting Judith's father. He would have respected himself more if he'd been able to put a hand that didn't tremble on the doorbell. His relief when Judith herself opened the door seemed to him to be cowardly.

Judith was looking incredibly beautiful. The magenta jersey wool dress she was wearing set off her unusual fairness and made her look much older and more sophisticated. The tone of the material gave colour to her cheeks and despite the scene with her father at the breakfast-table, she still had that appearance of well-being she had acquired on her Christmas holiday.

As always when he first saw her after a brief absence, Rocky's desire to possess her stifled all other thought; but now, even her loveliness could not prevent the strange wish to run away.

'Please let's go quickly, Rocky,' Judith was saying, reaching for the beaver-lamb coat hanging on the hall-stand, and picking up her bag. 'Father may be home any moment. Fortunately, he's had to stay late at the bank.'

They climbed into the old Morris and Rocky realized that he must say something. So far he had not addressed a word to her. Foolishly, the only thing he could think of was:

'I'm terribly sorry, Judith!'

Olive Bryant had told her daughter that her father had been on the phone to Mr. Rockingham. She'd been terribly worried all day, wondering what her father had said.

If only she had had more self-control, she would never have blurted out that she might be having Rocky's baby.

She looked at Rocky tentatively.

'I do hope Father wasn't rude. I'm afraid he was in a towering rage.'

Rocky drew in his breath.

He said, almost aggressively:

'You needn't be afraid that I'll run out on you, Judith. After all, the whole thing's probably my fault, anyway.'

Judith gave him a quick, anxious glance.

'So you do know!' she whispered.

He nodded.

'Your father was hardly likely to keep quiet under the circumstances,' he said bitterly. 'And naturally, Dad's trying to persuade me not to rush into marriage just because of . . . because you might be going to have a child.'

He finished his sentence with difficulty.

'But it might never come to that,' Judith said.

Misunderstanding her, Rocky said in surprised relief:

'You mean you wouldn't expect me to marry you?'

Judith was stunned. Was this how Rocky looked on the possibility of marriage? Had the idea begun to frighten him, now that there seemed a likelihood that her father might give his consent?

'Of course, I *would* marry you, Judith, if there was going to be a baby.'

'You mean, you'll marry me if you *have* to?' The words were out before she could prevent them.

Rocky looked away from her, uncomfortably aware of the desperate hurt in her voice.

'No, no, I didn't mean that. I only meant that if there isn't anything to force us to get married just yet, then I think it would be more sensible to wait a few years. After all, Judith, it's not unreasonable of Dad to insist that I finish my apprenticeship and pass my exams and all that. He thinks I wouldn't be able to concentrate on my work if we were married, and I've got to get on, Judith, for your sake as much as mine.'

In that moment, Judith realized the true quality of the man she loved. She knew now that he was unsure of himself; weak; easily influenced by other people. It was obvious that his father had been working on him, and it looked as if he was succeeding in what he hoped to do.

Maybe Rocky's father was right. Maybe they should never have thought about marriage in the first place, and just been content to go about together and have a good time.

She felt a moment of bitter resentment at the unfairness of things. After all, it had been Rocky who insisted upon their elopement. If her father hadn't followed them to Scotland, they'd have been married now and Rocky might actually be regretting it!

Only pride prevented her from voicing the despair in her heart. While the cry within her said: 'You don't love me. You don't need me the way I need you,' her lips were saying, quietly:

'It's all right, Rocky, it really doesn't matter very much. You're probably right anyway. We're both far too young.'

Rocky grabbed at her last words.

'That's just it, Judith. We are awfully

young, and as Dad said, how can we possibly be sure that we'll still want each other ten, twenty or thirty years from now? It's best to wait and to be sure. Best for you, too, Judith.'

She knew that it was all over, and now nothing mattered but that this conversation should come to an end. Nothing Rocky might say could alter the fact that he didn't love her. Perhaps he'd never really loved her. If you loved a person, you had no doubts about the future. She had never once questioned whether or not she would still love Rocky in ten or twenty years' time. It was passion, and not love, which died with the passing of time.

She wondered if Rocky had forgotten the baby, *his* baby; and as suddenly realized that she didn't want Rocky to marry her just because of that. It would be quite intolerable . . . she'd rather face the consequences alone. She didn't want Rocky's pity in place of his love. Because of this, she said:

'You needn't look so worried, Rocky.

We don't have to get married now, as I'm not going to have a baby.'

He looked as if a burden had been lifted from his shoulders. He was in fact so relieved that he said:

'Well, in that case, Judith, there's really no reason why we shouldn't go on as we are.'

He was unprepared for her violent rejoinder:

'No, Rocky. I think it's best if we don't see each other, at least for a while. It will give us both a chance to look at the whole affair more objectively and find out what we really do feel about each other.' The sarcasm which edged her voice escaped him when she added:

'As you say, we're both very young, and we may change.'

Rocky could hardly believe that he had won his freedom so easily. He knew his father would be delighted, and enormously relieved. He, too, felt relief, but something more besides — dismay that all the plans he and Judith had made, all the wonderful times together, everything they had been to one another, could be dissolved in a brief half-hour of time. He felt, subconsciously, that their parting, if this was really to be it, should be more dramatic. It might have seemed more real if Judith had been crying, had clung to him, and told him she couldn't bear not to see him again.

'You can't really mean that, Judy. We can't just part as if we didn't mean anything to each other. Especially as there's no reason to do so — ' He broke off, unhappily aware that she wasn't willing to compromise. Either he must be prepared to marry her at once, or he must lose her. Crazy as it seemed, he'd been sure when he went to Gretna, yet he wasn't sure of himself now.

If only Judith would let things drift . . . but she was sitting, stiff-backed with her hands folded together like a little girl at a tea-party, and she seemed unapproachable.

'You might as well take me home

now, Rocky. There really isn't anything else to say,' she told him in a matter-of-fact, emotionless voice.

'But the cinema — ' Rocky began to protest.

'If you don't mind awfully, Rocky, I've a bit of a headache,' Judith broke in sharply. 'Shall we go?'

If this was to be goodbye he would have liked to kiss her, but her tone of voice, her manner — all kept him at bay. Suddenly angry with her, his heart strangely uneasy, he switched on the engine and in silence drove her home.

She insisted that he should leave her at the end of the drive and since he didn't wish to see her father he didn't argue the point. She climbed out of the car and shut the door, calling a quick 'Goodbye, Rocky,' and a moment later she disappeared into the house.

Nonplussed, he waited only a few seconds and then, with a shrug of his shoulders, turned the car and drove it slowly home.

Judith waited for the back light to

disappear into the distance, and then slipped out through the front door and began to walk back in the direction from which they had come. There were few people in the streets and the night air hung frostily in the lamplights. But she was not aware of the cold. Her mind had become numbed by too much emotion, too much tension, building up to this evening with the dreadful shock of discovering Rocky's real feelings for her.

She walked away from the house, afraid to face her father's angry disappointment or her mother's tearful questioning. It didn't matter very much where she went, so long as it was away from home — provided she could be alone.

11

Judith walked on, oblivious as to where her feet were taking her. Once or twice, someone passed her in the street but she did not see them. Without conscious thought, she counted the street lamps, her eyes were fastening on the one ahead until she had walked through the pool of light beneath and then she would look up again to the next one.

'Good heavens, Judith! Whatever are you doing here at this time of night?'

She was aware she had bumped into somebody, and a second later, realized that it was Gavin.

'I was walking!' she said stupidly.

'To the surgery? But you've passed it,' Gavin replied. 'I'm just on my way there myself. I must have left my favourite pipe — ' he broke off, puzzled by the strange expression on Judith's face.

'Is anything wrong?' he asked.

She looked at him, blankly and uncomprehendingly. He took her arm, turned her round, and led her back to the surgery door. The complete lack of resistance, and her silence, further convinced him that she must have undergone some kind of shock. Unlocking the door, he took her into the surgery and pushed her into a chair while he knelt down and put a match to the gas-fire. He waited till the warm glow filled the room, and then he pulled up a chair beside her and taking one little ice-cold hand in his own, he tried to rub some warmth into her. Her face was completely expressionless, and she stared ahead of her as if she was quite unaware of her surroundings, or of him.

Growing ever more concerned about her, he replaced her hand in her lap and went through to the lobby adjoining the waiting room where there was a gas-ring on which Judith would make their morning coffee. There was no milk, but fortunately he found the coffee-tin and sugar and within five minutes he was carrying two steaming cups of black coffee through to the other room.

'Drink it, Judith. It'll warm you up.'

She sipped obediently and gasped a little as the hot liquid burned her mouth. Gavin put down his own cup and took her hand again.

'Now tell me what's happened,' he commanded quietly.

Judith turned her face slowly to his and in a quiet, remote little voice said:

'It's all over. I shan't be seeing Rocky again.'

Gavin drew in his breath sharply. So that was it, he thought grimly. There'd been some row, and the boy had walked out on her . . . Quickly, he sought to comfort her.

'Words are never irrevocable, Judith. You can always ring him up and tell him you didn't mean it. He'll forgive you, and you'll look back on this for what it really is, just a lovers' tiff.'

Judith's small toneless voice corrected his emotionlessly.

'I'll never see him again. He doesn't love me. I suppose I've known for some time but I didn't want to face facts.'

Quite suddenly, her eyes filled with tears, which spilled over and rolled down her cheeks. Her crying was completely noiseless, as if she were crying in spite of herself. He began to feel a real anxiety for her now. Something in the calm statement of fact convinced him she spoke the truth, and yet he couldn't believe that any young man in his right senses could throw over a girl like Judith. He recalled with a sudden sense of shock her condition.

Good God, he thought, the boy couldn't have walked out on her *now*! No wonder she was like this. She ought to be home in bed with a sedative. Impulsively, he told her so.

'I can't go home. I don't want to go home. *Please don't make me.*'

Gavin got up and paced the floor. He was beginning to understand at last just how serious this all was. He could very well guess the atmosphere of Victorian disapproval there must be awaiting her at home. From all Judith had said about her father, Gavin could guess that Bryant would rather see his daughter married, however unhappily, than in disgrace. And that was how he and Judith's mother would look upon this — as a disgrace she had brought upon them as well as upon herself. Condemnation was not what she needed at the moment; it was comfort, understanding, security. And who was there to offer these to her? As far as he knew, Judith had no other relatives. She had once told him that her father's career in the bank had necessitated frequent transfers around the country and that the family had no very close friends in Yeovil.

Looking back on Judith's life, Gavin realized that it must have been practically devoid of love and companionship — or at least until she had fallen in love with Rocky. He could understand how a girl like Judith, emotionally starved, must have given her whole overflowing heart into this first affair. Even her physical surrender after that unsuccessful elopement was a natural reaction and one for which he couldn't blame her. And now she was going to have to pay the full price for the unrestrained quality of her love.

He was suddenly aware that she was talking, even while the tears still rolled down her cheeks.

' . . . so the baby ought to have made everything turn out all right, as you once said, Gavin. Father would give his consent now. But what I never thought about was how Rocky's parents and — and Rocky — would react.'

Gavin stared at the small, white profile, aghast. He had been the one to say to her: 'You hold the trump card.' He had spoken unthinkingly, never realizing that she might take him seriously. He'd meant only to comfort her after the unsuccessful elopement and lighten the tension of the moment. She *couldn't* have started the baby intentionally.

He sat down heavily in the chair at his desk, and tried to calm the hurried beating of his heart. There was only one solution. Since Rocky wouldn't — he, Gavin, must marry her. In a way, he was responsible for the predicament she was in, and it would solve all her problems. Of course, she didn't love him, but that needn't matter. He'd be able to take care of her — and the child — and he recalled with pleasure the fact that he was now in a financial position to do this. It wasn't such a bad idea, anyway. Although he'd long since grown accustomed to his bachelor existence, he'd often longed for a real home of his own; a house such as Rosemary's which, unlike his own box-like rooms, seemed lived-in and cared-for, and a haven to return to by comparison.

Remembering Rosemary, he thought of her words to him at the end of the Christmas holiday: 'Now if only you'd find yourself some nice girl like Judith, Gavin, and settle down . . .'

Yes, Rosemary had liked Judith immensely and so had Phil. Gavin warmed to the idea of sharing his life with Judith. They'd always made a go of it at work. Judith seemed to have an uncanny knack of anticipating his moods and wishes, and making his life generally much easier. And she never irritated or annoyed him. Why shouldn't they get along just as well on a domestic footing? They might even be very happy together.

His eye caught the photograph of Helen on his desk and he frowned slightly. Of course, he'd have to stop seeing Helen. No more 'lost week-ends' in Town. But surprisingly, the thought didn't cause him the slightest regret. Helen was attractive and amusing, but never what he'd wanted in a wife, whereas Judith . . .

He looked across at the girl's bowed head with an unexpected rush of tenderness. She was so young, and defenceless, and hurt. She roused in him all the 'best' in his nature; unlike Helen, who merely appealed to him physically.

He pulled himself up sharply. It was one thing deciding in his own mind that he wanted to marry Judith; but supposing she refused to marry him? Quite suddenly it mattered terribly that she should agree. He went across to her, and raised her gently in the chair, his hand beneath the small pointed chin so that she was forced to look up at him.

'Judith, I want you to marry me. I want you to let me look after you. You will say yes, won't you?'

Gavin's proposal penetrated her mind, slowly. The barrier of numbness that had enshrouded her until now suddenly dissolved. The kindness in his voice, and the generosity of his offer, was more than she could bear. She buried her face against the rough tweed jacket as she had done once before, and sobbed noisily now, like a young child.

He held her tightly, his cheek against the smooth silken hair, aware of strange pain around his heart, part tenderness, part pity, and part something else to which as yet he could give no name.

'Don't darling, please don't cry,' he whispered, using the endearment unconsciously. 'I'll take care of you. You needn't even go home if you don't want to. You can go and stay with Rosemary — she'd love to have you. It's all right, darling, *everything's going to be all right.*'

Gradually her sobs quietened and the convulsive trembling of her slim, young body calmed. Reason returned to her troubled mind, and following the single moment of relief and gratitude for all this man was so unexpectedly offering her, came the knowledge that she couldn't possibly take advantage of it.

She tried to tell him so, but Gavin would not listen.

'It's what I want for myself, too,' he told her. 'Don't ask me how I know, Judith, but I feel deep down inside me that this would be right — for both of us. I don't expect you to decide this minute, but I'm sure once you can look at things calmly again, you'll see that it's a wonderful plan for both of us. I want a home, a wife, children — and you need someone to look after you and the baby. Don't refuse me now, Judith. Just think about it.'

White-faced, Judith said guiltily:

'You mustn't think Rocky has walked out on his responsibilities, Gavin. It's all my fault, really. You see, once I knew he didn't love me, I told him there wasn't going to be a baby.'

Gavin raised his eyebrows.

'Then I don't think so badly of him. You've a right to your pride, Judith, and I admire you for giving the boy a chance to back out, if that's what he really wanted. But you don't need to feel you must protect me, too. I'm old enough to know what I want and what I'm doing. I want to marry you, Judith — I think we might make each other happy.'

He glanced swiftly at the watch on his wrist and saw that it was ten o'clock.

With an excitement that was quite foreign to his usual calm nature, he said:

'I'm going to drive you down to Rosemary's tonight. I'll ring Rosemary and tell her we're coming; then I'm going home with you. I want to talk to your father.'

'Father!' Judith drew in her breath quickly. She dreaded the mere thought of his angry, disappointed face when he learned that she and Rocky would never be married, now. Would her father let her go to Gavin's sister?

As if she had spoken her fears aloud, Gavin was saying:

'You needn't worry about your father, Judith. I know how I'll handle him. I'll talk to him while you go and pack an over-night bag.'

He was so happy that she was offering no resistance, that he decided not to give her time for second thoughts. He lifted the telephone and asked for Rosemary's number.

The conversation lasted only a few moments. Rosemary asked no questions and merely told him she would have the spare room ready.

Harold Bryant, however, greeted him with a torrent of questions. Briefly, Gavin told him what had happened.

'There is no need for you to upset yourself, sir. With your permission, I intend to take your daughter to stay with my married sister. There is no one there to link Judith's name with yours and if she is in fact having this baby, I'm sure you would infinitely prefer that she should not remain in this district . . .'

As he had imagined, this line of argument was one which instantly struck a responsive chord in the other man's mind.

'And further, to relieve your mind,' Gavin went on, 'I think I ought to inform you that I'm hoping very much that your daughter will agree to marry me.'

He smiled wryly at the sudden change of tone in Bryant's voice.

'My dear young man, I never knew — Judith never said — of course she has always spoken very highly of you and she's always loved her work. Very kind indeed of your sister to have Judith. I confess I don't fully understand how this has all come about. I thought Judith was out with Rockingham this evening. But no matter, it looks as if everything might turn out for the best, after all.'

In a way, Gavin could understand Bryant's predicament. Judith was his only child, and all this must have been a terrible shock to him; the more so, perhaps, since he was nearer the age to be Judith's grandfather than parent.

Judith came downstairs with her suitcase and Gavin told her quickly that everything had been fixed up. She had made some attempt to renew her face with a light make-up and he was gratified to see a faint smile on her lips and relief flash into her eyes at his words. He hurried her through a quick goodbye to her parents, and out to his car.

'You're being wonderfully kind,' she said quietly. 'And your sister, too. I feel awful, thinking of the trouble I'm putting everyone to. Will you be able to stay there too, Gavin?'

He shook his head.

'It's a bit late to cancel tomorrow morning's surgery, but don't let that worry you, my dear. An hour's drive is nothing. I'll come back tonight and then run down again after lunch tomorrow, as we've lots to talk about.'

Judith said:

'You think of everything, Gavin. You can't begin to know how grateful I am. A week-end with Rosemary would put me on my feet and I'll be quite all right by Monday. I feel rather bad that you should have to cope with a Saturday surgery.'

'You're on indefinite leave, Judith,' Gavin said firmly, 'and by that I mean that you're going to stay at Cherry Tree Farm for as long as I can persuade you to. If necessary, I shall get a temporary replacement in the surgery until the future is more decided. After all you've been through, you're going to need several weeks of rest and care, and if you don't mind about your health for yourself, you must consider your baby.'

Judith had forgotten the baby and only now did she realize the enormity of Gavin's offer to marry her. Of course, it was out of the question, but she'd always be grateful that he had offered.

'Oh, Gavin!' she whispered helplessly. 'You're trying to make everything easy for me. But it can't be quite so simple as you make out. For one thing, I can't marry you. It isn't just because I'm still in love with Rocky, in spite of everything; it's because it just wouldn't be fair to you. You'd only regret it if I said 'yes'. Besides, what about Helen?'

Gavin raised his eyebrows.

'Well, what about Helen? She and I have had some good times together but that's as far as it goes, Judith. I thought I was in love with her once, but she's the last person in the world I would think of marrying.'

Judith looked so surprised that he was forced to add:

'Did you think we were engaged?'

Judith told him, briefly, of that hour's meeting with Helen — could it really be this same day? she thought, with surprise. She explained that Helen hadn't mentioned an engagement, but she'd inferred in all that she said that it might not be long before she and Gavin were married. Judith tried to remember Helen's exact words and could not.

'Perhaps I misunderstood!' she said. 'It was just an impression that — '

'Well, you can forget about it,' Gavin broke in. 'And while we're on the subject of Helen, I think I ought to tell you, Judith, that there has been an occasion when Helen and I spent the night at her flat. I don't suppose I need say more. But there's never been any question of marriage, and I'm sure Helen doesn't expect it.'

'But I liked her!' Judith stated inconsequently. 'She was terribly kind to me, Gavin. She offered to help Rocky and me if . . . ' her voice broke slightly, ' . . . if Rocky was willing to elope with me again.'

Gavin frowned. There was something odd here he did not fully understand, but there was no time now to go into it. Judith looked desperately white and tired. The thing to do was to get her to the farm and safely tucked up in bed.

Judith was, in fact, so tired that she fell asleep, her fair head leaning against his shoulder. Gavin drove stiffly, trying not to move too much lest he should wake her.

Once again he experienced that queer mixture of pain and happiness, which he explained away as tenderness for her. She seemed so small and helpless and childlike, and it hurt him to think of all she had gone through, and still had to go through. Seventeen was young enough to start suffering, he thought, remembering his own experiences when he'd been but a year older. His had been both physical and mental torture, and he'd never doubted which was the harder to bear.

When they arrived at the farm, he

carried her, protesting sleepily, into the house. Rosemary gave him one look of surprise and then, tactful as always, led him straight upstairs to the spare room which once again was warm and welcoming in the firelight. When Gavin had gone, she helped Judith undress and popped her into bed as she might have done one of her own children. She asked no questions and told Judith, when she tried to offer her thanks, that she was to go to sleep and they could discuss everything in the morning. She went downstairs and joined Gavin and Phil who were having a whisky in the drawing-room.

'She's almost asleep. She looks exhausted, Gavin. Are we allowed to know what's happened?'

Normally, Gavin would not have dreamed of betraying a confidence, but he knew any secret was absolutely safe with Rosemary and his brother-in-law. Also he felt it was essential that they should know the true situation, since it was now up to Rosemary to cope with

Judith. He wanted his sister's support, too, and was surprised when she shook her head vehemently at his suggestion of marriage.

'No, Gavin! I know you're fond of Judith, and sorry for her. But that's no basis for a successful and happy marriage. The baby doesn't matter. I'm willing to accept that *you* could tolerate another man's child if you loved its mother enough; but without love, no, no, *no*!'

For a moment there was complete silence in the room. No one spoke until Gavin said slowly, almost as if he were talking to himself:

'But I really wouldn't mind. It would be Judith's child, and — ' He broke off, suddenly realizing exactly what he wanted to say. To his surprise the words formed on his lips, and he heard himself say, firmly: ' . . . and I *do* love her. I suppose that sounds crazy to you both. To tell you the truth, I've only just realized it myself. But it's true, nevertheless. I know Judith is years younger than I am and no doubt I seem old and dull to her, but I think that, given time, she might become fond of me. As for me — I can't think of anything I'd rather do than share my life with her.'

Rosemary looked at her adored younger brother with mixed feelings. She didn't doubt that Gavin believed what he was saying, but she wasn't convinced he had put the right interpretation on his feelings for Judith. Even as a little boy he'd always been deeply affected by the 'lame ducks', whether it was an animal with an injured foot or a little boy at school the other boys were teasing. Normally even-tempered and not in the least pugnacious, Gavin had rushed to the defence of the down-trodden and come home with a black eye or bleeding nose, usually dragging the unfortunate 'lame duck' with him. The trouble was, those he rescued invariably clung to him with pathetic devotion and Gavin had never known quite what to do with the love he had engendered but never really wanted when it was showered upon him. If Judith were to turn to Gavin on the rebound, wasn't it possible that exactly the same situation could arise and for Gavin to regret his chivalrous offer?

Rosemary went over to her brother, put a hand on his arm and said, gently:

'These things are never the better for being decided in a hurry, Gavin. Even if you're sure how *you* feel, it wouldn't be fair to Judith to rush her into any decision. For all you know, the boy may be regretting the fact that he's lost her. Sometimes it only needs a jolt like this to make the young come to their senses. If you were to tie Judith up now, she wouldn't be free if the boy she loves wants her back.'

'But he can't just pick her up and put her down as if she were a — a plaything!' Gavin protested angrily. 'He's no right to do so.'

'In a way he has, old boy,' Phil put in unexpectedly. 'After all, it is his child.'

Gavin looked thoroughly shaken. When Judith had said she never wished to see Rockingham again, he believed she meant it. He assumed the affair was all over and done with.

Phil asked him if he would like another whisky. Gavin shook his head.

'I've got to get back tonight because surgery starts at nine tomorrow and Saturday is usually my busiest day. But if I may, I'll be back after lunch tomorrow.'

Rosemary followed him to the front door, and reaching up, gave him a sisterly kiss.

'Don't worry, my dear. We'll look after your Judith. I'll have a long talk with her in the morning and see if I can find out what she really feels.'

Gavin did not hurry the journey home. He let his mind ramble at will and found that all his thoughts were of Judith. He could visualize her now, curled up like a small, lonely child in that large spare-room bed, and once again felt his heart constrict. He knew then, without any shadow of doubt, that he had fallen in love.

12

Helen replaced the telephone receiver on the table in her hotel bedroom with an angry little gesture of annoyance. It was really too bad — midnight, and Gavin still not home. Where on earth could he have got to? He'd made no mention at lunch that he was going away for the week-end. Could he have taken that little receptionist of his out for the night? Just what did Judith mean to him?

Helen was already undressed and in bed, but she knew she was unlikely to sleep with her body so tensed with thwarted ideas. She lit another cigarette and lay back on the pillow, puffing a cloud of smoke into the air. It was damnable not being able to get in touch with Gavin.

Helen had started on her way back to Town after leaving Judith but had gone little over twenty miles before her car had developed water-hub trouble which the garage could not repair at once. She took a taxi back into Yeovil and booked in at the hotel where she and Gavin had lunched. Since her arrival she had tried to telephone him at his house every hour but there was no reply.

She tried to console herself with the thought that he might be stuck out at some farm waiting for a cow to calve, or some emergency. She finally fell asleep, having reassured herself that he would surely be there in the morning.

She woke late and glancing at her watch tried to ring Gavin even before she ordered her breakfast in bed. His daily woman answered, and to Helen's irritation told her that Mr. Pelham had just left. Helen gave him five minutes to reach the surgery, only to be met once more with 'no reply'.

She poured a cup of coffee and drank it thoughtfully. Maybe it was just as well she'd not been able to reach Gavin yet. It was only just nine o'clock and the last thing in the world she wanted was to appear too eager. It would be far better to stroll casually into the surgery and to give the appearance of 'dropping-in' for another surprise visit.

Helen bathed, dressed and made up her face with even more than her usual care. She had no change of clothes but with her clever dress-sense she managed to make herself look more countryfied. She also changed her hair-style a little so that the sophisticated upswept pile of hair fell more softly round her face and made her look slightly more *jeune-fille*. At last satisfied with her appearance, she strolled out into the bright January sunshine and was glad that Gavin's surgery was only a few blocks away.

At first she thought the tall young man standing on the doorstep was Gavin, but as she came nearer she saw that it was a much older man, and only his height and clothes had misled her.

She walked past him and rang the surgery bell. The man behind her said:

'I've already rung twice. There

doesn't seem to be anybody there.'

Helen was puzzled. She'd taken at least an hour over her *toilette* and Gavin must surely have got here by now. And what about his assistant, Judith?

'Have you been waiting long?' she asked her companion.

'Since five-to-nine. I'd hoped to get my interview with Mr. Pelham before surgery started.'

Helen's curiosity quickened.

'Interview? You're not a client, then?'

The man shook his head.

'I'm a reporter from the *Western Echo*. Cigarette?'

He held out a packet of Senior Service and lit one for her with a quick, interested glance at Helen's beautiful face.

She didn't look as if she was 'local', he mused. He knew most of the people hereabouts and Helen was obviously a 'somebody'. His gossip column had covered nearly all the county families at various society functions, and with his memory for faces he knew he wouldn't have forgotten Helen had he seen her somewhere before.

He wasn't the only one who was summing-up. Helen, with her sharp mind had put two and two together and made four. She guessed the reporter had got wind of Gavin's inheritance. She had noted, too, his quick curious glance at her. She was used to the admiring glances of strange men, but this she felt was different. The reporter was out for news, and maybe she could supply it.

'Is Mr. Pelham expecting you?' She posed her question carefully.

'As a matter of fact, he's not. I tried to get hold of him yesterday evening but without success, and I thought if I were early enough this morning I might be lucky.'

Helen gave him a friendly smile.

'I presume you've heard, then, about the sudden death of Mr. Pelham's uncle? It was very unexpected, wasn't it?'

As she had anticipated, he fell for the bait.

'You know the family, then? You're not by any chance a relative of Mr. Pelham's?'

Helen looked down at her gloved hands.

'W-e-l-l, not exactly. At least, not yet . . . I mean . . . ' She broke off with an excellent pretence at confusion.

The reporter made up his mind quickly. Since he wasn't even sure that Mr. Pelham was going to grant him an interview, even if he did turn up, it might be worth his while getting some inside information from this woman.

'Would you think it presumptuous of me if I suggested we go across the road and have a cup of coffee whilst we're waiting?'

'Why, I'd love to,' Helen agreed at once. 'It's pretty cold standing here, despite the sunshine. But why not come back to my hotel? It'll be a lot more comfortable there than in the teashop, and warmer too.'

They walked back to Helen's hotel and were soon sitting in the lounge with a coffee-tray between them.

The reporter was delighted to find that he had only to prompt Helen a little here and there, to acquire a great deal of information about Pelham — the fact that he'd been a prisoner in Korea and, although Helen couldn't tell him why, had been awarded the D.S.O. on his return; how he'd built up his practice after qualifying with honours at the Royal College of Veterinary Surgeons. To his question as to whether Gavin might sell up and go out to Kenya, Helen replied:

'I can only give my personal opinion, but I doubt very much whether he'll leave England. I think he plans to settle down in the country somewhere.'

Once again he nibbled at the bait.

'Would it be impertinent to enquire if the 'settling-down' is to be with you?'

He had already discovered that Helen was a model, and knew that he had the makings of a very good story here — 'Local Vet. inherits title and fortune and marries model-girl.' It would certainly liven up the old columns of the

Echo. Helen was smiling enigmatically.

'Your question puts me in rather an awkward position. Nothing has been definitely arranged, but . . . '

'But that's good enough for me,' the man thought, with satisfaction. There had to be a girl in the picture somewhere. A glamorous model would nicely fill the bill.

He wondered whether he should go back and try to see Pelham, and decided against it. He could always follow up this story with a personal interview when the amount of Pelham's inheritance became known. That might be a good line to take with regard to the woman. '*Will Baronet Wed Beautiful Model Now He Has Come Into His Fortune?*' Or dare he go further than that? '*Baronet To Wed Beautiful Model Soon.*'

He turned to Helen and said, persuasively:

'The last thing in the world I want to do is to make things awkward for you, but I'm sure you'll understand my point. I'd like to run an article on Mr.

Pelham — or should I say Sir Gavin Pelham — beginning perhaps like this: '*Today I spoke to the beautiful model-girl Helen Rowe, who tells me that her fiancé, Mr. Gavin Pelham, has recently become a Baronet on the death of his uncle in Kenya*' . . . ' He paused, waiting for her reaction.

For a moment, Helen did not reply. It was obvious that her exact relationship with Gavin was of interest to the reporter — come to that, to her, too! But did she dare let it be implied that she and Gavin were engaged? If the article were printed, she could of course deny that she'd said they were engaged. There was nothing in writing, and if Gavin chose to take it up with the reporter it would of course be her word against his. She could tell Gavin the man had jumped to the conclusion, and express her regret. Gavin might even welcome the opening she'd given him, and propose. It was just such a scheme as this which had been at the back of her mind ever since she'd found herself talking to a newspaper reporter. She chided herself for hesitating when there was so much at stake. This might turn out to be a very good way to achieve her aims.

'So long as you understand that Mr. Pelham and I aren't officially engaged . . .' she muttered.

He asked her a few more questions about her background and her career, and persuaded her without any difficulty to submit to a few photographs in the hotel garden.

By the time he left, it was nearly lunch-time and Helen decided to try again to contact Gavin. Once again, the daily woman answered:

'I'm very sorry, madam. Mr. Pelham's been in but he's gone again. That is, he came in for a quick lunch and then packed his bag and rushed off, saying he wouldn't be back till Sunday night. I *think* he said as how he was going to his sister's.'

Helen replaced the receiver, swearing under her breath as she did so. She couldn't possibly follow him, uninvited, to his sister's home. It was really damn bad luck, she thought. Then her frown changed to a complacent smile as she remembered the reporter. Her extra night in Yeovil had not been entirely wasted. As things had turned out, her interview might prove a lot more profitable than a meeting with Gavin. Realizing that it was pointless now to remain in Yeovil, she paid her bill and ordered a taxi to the garage, but before leaving the hotel she paid the girl at the desk to forward her a copy of the *Western Evening Echo* as soon as it was on sale.

13

It was very quiet and peaceful in the drawing-room at Cherry Tree Farm. The children were out in the garden with Phil, the baby warmly wrapped in her pram where she could watch the others playing. Indoors, Judith lay on the sofa with a soft mohair rug over her legs. Gavin and Rosemary sat opposite her, Gavin smoking his pipe and Rosemary knitting a jersey for little April.

Judith felt so lethargic that she had been willing for Rosemary to fuss over her and treat her like a convalescent child. It was very comforting to lie here, staring into the firelight, no longer minding much about anything.

'Feeling all right?' Gavin asked anxiously. She smiled and nodded her head.

'I've never felt quite like this before,' she said. 'I feel detached from myself, as if nothing really matters very much any more. At least, not here.' She placed her hand with a simple little gesture over her heart. 'My mind isn't confused and I can think quite clearly about everything that's happened. I can see, for instance, that I've behaved very stupidly. I can even see that my father is right, in a way. Rocky isn't grown-up yet. He's only a boy and it would be quite unfair to tie him down to anything so permanent as marriage.'

Gavin was careful not to interrupt. He knew, just as Rosemary did, that so long as she didn't keep her thoughts bottled up inside her, it would be better for her.

Judith gave them both a quick, shy smile.

'I suppose you think I'm very extroverted to be talking like this. Somehow it's so much easier talking to you than talking to my family. You've both been so wonderful to me that you seem like very old friends.'

Rosemary put down her knitting and stood up.

'I'm glad you feel like that, Judith. And before I go out I want to say that Phil and I were discussing you last night and we both agreed that we'd like to offer you a job and a permanent home here. I know things aren't too good between you and your parents and if you think you'd like to live with us I could badly do with someone to help me with the children. No, don't make up your mind yet. Think about it first, and then let me know what you decide.'

Judith was touched by Rosemary's kindness and her voice trembled a little as she said to Gavin, once they were alone:

'You're all so wonderful to me. I've been so lucky to find such good friends as you and Rosemary and Phil, too. Do you really think they want me here, Gavin? I do so dread the thought of going home, and yet, I want to be able to go on working for you, too.'

Gavin thought how much he would miss her daily presence in the surgery with him. He hated the thought of some other girl sitting at her desk. He would be forced to get a replacement. This morning had proved it. But he didn't voice these feelings. Above all, he wanted her to reach her own decision about the future without influence from him.

Judith said suddenly:

'Even if Rocky wanted to marry me now, I should say no. I've always believed that it is wrong to marry without love and I doubt very much that Rocky truly loves me. I'm even beginning to doubt that I'm in love with him.'

Gavin could not control the swift throb of hope that swelled his heart so that he could not speak. If it were only true . . .

'Last night I thought my heart was broken,' Judith went on. 'Now, I'm lying here quite content without Rocky and not even sure that I ever want to see him again.'

Gavin was not made of steel. He had truly intended not to confuse her by telling of his own love for her, but with this new slender ray of hope his self-control broke. With a quick, impulsive movement, he was across the room and sitting beside her on the big chintz-covered sofa. He took her two small hands in his, forcing her to look directly into his face.

'Oh, Judith, I do love you so much. I know I shouldn't be saying this, not now. I promised myself that I wouldn't. But I can't help myself. I've never been in love before. Twice I thought I was, and now I realize that I didn't understand even the meaning of the word. I think I must have loved you ever since that day you came to the surgery for an interview. I'd never meant to employ anyone so young and inexperienced. Yet I found myself saying 'Yes, the job's yours', without any logical reason for doing so. What shakes me now is the thought that we've spent nearly a year in each other's company and I never realized I loved you until last night.'

Judith did not try to withdraw her

hands. Gavin's grasp was warm and firm and immensely comforting. She felt curiously close to him in spirit. She could understand what he meant — all those weeks of working together and he'd meant no more to her than a pleasant, kindly employer whom she respected and admired. It was only recently she'd begun to see him as a friend. And now, at last, as a man.

She did not doubt the sincerity of his love. In many ways, Gavin was reserved and slow to make up his mind. Last night she had thought his offer to marry her was made from a sense of responsibility, or pity, or just kindness; but now, looking into his eyes, she could read only love there. She was at once flattered, confused, strangely excited by the knowledge that a man of Gavin's age could feel this way about her. It almost made her relationship with Rocky seem like a child's game. With sudden, startling, feminine curiosity, she wondered how she would feel if Gavin kissed her. Her romantic mind told her that if she were truly in love with Rocky, she couldn't bear the thought of another man's lips on hers, yet she wanted Gavin to kiss her. She sat silently, her hands loose in Gavin's grasp, trying to sort out her bewildering emotions. Since her arrival here, everything had taken on a completely new aura. It was almost as if there were two Judiths; the girl who lived at home, young, childish, silly — and the woman who sat here in the warm firelight with Gavin, wondering what it would be like to be kissed.

Something warm and expectant in Judith's expression gave Gavin an instinctive understanding of her thoughts. He leant forward, meaning only to touch her lips gently with his own, but he had not counted on the sudden intoxication of her proximity. He no longer thought that this was Judith, a mere child to be cared for and gentled. The girl he held in his arms had become a woman, soft, exciting, desirable.

His arms tightened round her, and as her lips parted in sudden unexpected responsiveness, he crushed her to him with a longing he had never experienced before. Her arms were round his neck now and he could feel her heart pounding against his. His mind thrilled with the knowledge that she wanted him as much as he wanted her.

For one brief moment, Judith began to struggle. She had a moment's horrified memory of this same wild abandon on Rocky's face as he made love to her in the car.

She didn't want it to be like that! she thought wildly. But as Gavin kissed her again she knew that because this was Gavin, everything was quite, quite different. He was holding her gently now, stroking the long fair hair with soothing, tender hands. Now, perversely, she wanted him to kiss her again. To take her back in his arms and hold her so closely that nothing in the world mattered but his nearness. She gave a little cry and catching hold of his hand she laid her cheek against it, feeling a moment of deep tenderness which she did not try to explain. Gavin sat back in the sofa and turned her round so that she was leaning with her back against him, her head against his shoulder. He laughed shakily, and said:

'Comfortable, darling!'

There was so much love in his voice, Judith felt her heart begin to beat more swiftly again. And she couldn't understand her feelings. Only a day ago she had believed her heart was broken because Rocky didn't love her. And here she was, in Gavin's arms, forced to admit to herself that his kisses stirred her far more deeply than Rocky's had ever done.

'You mustn't frown, my love!' She felt the quick soft touch of his lips against her forehead and heard him say: 'There's nothing to worry about, and please, Judith, don't regret what's just happened.'

She turned her head and looked up at him. The trusting innocence of her eyes caught at his heart.

'I don't regret it, Gavin. I just don't

understand how — how I could like it so much.'

He smiled.

'I expect it's rebound!' he said gently. 'A perfectly normal reaction, Judith.'

She pondered his words seriously. It was true that there was immense comfort from his love and the knowledge that he found her attractive. Rocky's rejection had been a blow to her pride as well as to her heart.

Gavin tried to convince himself that what he'd just told Judith was true. But if this were no more than rebound, he argued with himself, she shouldn't be here lying contentedly against his shoulder, soft and responsive and relaxed.

He knew he ought to be regretting that mad, impulsive embrace and yet he could feel only a great happiness and hope. He no longer had the smallest doubt that he was madly in love with her. He'd ceased even to think of her as the small, helpless, hurt child who needed his protection and comfort. She was now so much more, a woman who attracted him in a way Helen had never been able to do. He understood at last how desire, heightened and sweetened by love, could together become tremendous, overpowering emotion — greater than anything he'd ever known before.

'I wish we could stay here always!' Judith said, suddenly. 'I wish we could just make time stand still. I don't know why, but I'm completely happy and I'd like it to be like this always. I don't want there to be a tomorrow.'

Precious as the moment was, it could not spell complete happiness to Gavin. There could be no peace for him now until he knew that Judith loved him — until, in fact, she was his wife.

'Marry me!' His voice was so soft that she barely caught the words. 'Marry me, and it could be like this always, Judith.'

She made no reply. If she could only believe what he said, how simple everything would be. But there was Rocky and the baby. She knew she couldn't forget the past, however much she might want to.

There was a sudden noise as the children came running in from the garden, chattering in their small, high-pitched voices. With a sigh, Gavin released Judith and went back to his chair on the other side of the fireplace. A moment or two later, Rosemary opened the door and announced:

'Tea's nearly ready. We're having a family meal in the kitchen. So five minutes more.'

Phil followed almost immediately, and flopped into the winged chair with the evening paper. He glanced through the sports results, and then turned to the front page, and gave a quick gasp of surprise.

'Great Scot, Gavin! This is all about you!'

Gavin jumped up and leant across the back of Phil's chair, looking over his shoulder. The first thing that caught his eye was Helen's faintly-smiling face, with her head tilted slightly back against a stone wall. Then his eye caught the big bold print, staggering him with its import: '*Local Vet. Becomes a Baronet. Soon To Wed Beautiful Model Girl, Helen Rowe — pictured above.*'

The article went on to give details of his uncle's death and a slightly exaggerated impression of the size of his uncle's coffee plantations in Kenya. It then gave brief details of his service in Korea, and finally — Gavin was forced to read the paragraph twice before he could believe what it said — '*We understand that Sir Gavin Pelham is unlikely to emigrate to Kenya and that he will probably settle down in this country with beautiful Helen Rowe. Readers may have seen her picture on magazine covers and in fashion magazines . . .*'

There was quite a bit more about Helen's modelling career but Gavin did not read it. He grabbed the paper from Phil's hand and strode through to the kitchen, thrusting it at his sister.

'Look, Rosemary, just look! God knows how the reporter got on to Helen. But not only has she given him plenty of personal details about me but she's actually told him we're engaged.'

He was so angry, he couldn't stand still while she read the article. Rosemary protested mildly.

'Don't get so worked up, Gavin. I've been wondering when there'd be something in the local papers about Uncle Basil's death. It was bound to come out. As for your girl-friend, I daresay she's quite innocent. You know what these reporters are; they jump to conclusions.'

'But good God, Rosemary, they can't print facts which aren't true. I could sue them for libel. Anyway, I don't see how our local reporter even knew of Helen's existence.'

As far as Gavin knew, Helen was in London and she'd certainly not given any interview to the press yesterday, unless she'd done so after seeing Judith.

He took the paper from Rosemary

and marched back with it into the drawing-room, putting it down on Judith's lap.

'You don't know anything about this, do you, Judith?'

He was still furiously angry, but his voice was gentler now. He waited while she read the article, and then asked her:

'Nobody came to the surgery while Helen was talking to you?'

Judith shook her head.

'There wasn't even a phone call, Gavin. Miss Rowe said she was going straight back to London.'

He caught the note of distress in her voice, and regardless of Phil's presence sat down beside her and took her hand.

'You realize it's not true, Judith? The bit about Helen, I mean. We've never been engaged, and as far as I know I've never given her the slightest reason for supposing that I intended to marry her.'

Judith's suggestion that he get in touch with the paper and tell them to correct their facts barely calmed him at all.

'But, Judith, what is your father going to think?'

'Father? I don't understand.'

Gavin's grey eyes betrayed his concern.

'I told him I wanted to marry you. I think it was chiefly because I did so that he let me bring you down here last night. He's hardly likely to let you stay here with Rosemary after reading this,' and he flicked the paper angrily with his hand.

Phil put in quietly:

'That article doesn't bind you to Helen Rowe in any way that I can see. I should think the best thing for you to do is to ring the *Echo* on Monday and make them deny it. Or if you'd like me to act as your solicitor and do it for you, I'd be only too pleased.'

Gavin relaxed, and then looked apologetic.

'Sorry I blew my top. It's just that none of it makes sense. I can't believe Helen could have done it *intentionally*, and yet — ' He broke off suddenly, uncertain of Helen. That unexpected visit yesterday, for instance. He'd taken it for granted at the time and yet, now it did seem a bit coincidental. But why? She wasn't in love with him.

'Perhaps she's after your money!'

Phil spoke jestingly, but at once Gavin knew that the missing piece of the jigsaw had fallen into place. Of course, of course! Why hadn't he thought of it before. It was only since Helen had heard of his uncle's death that her manner had changed. She'd always been quite open in the past about her determination to marry money.

'Good God! So that's it!'

'Oh, no, Gavin,' Judith protested. 'I can't believe such a thing about Miss Rowe. I know she's terribly fond of you — she told me so.'

Gavin swung round, his grey eyes blazing.

'You don't know the real Helen. And there's something else I'm beginning to understand, too — her interest in you.

Don't you see, Judith, with that peculiar feminine instinct of hers, she guessed you might come between her and what she wanted, and *that's* why she took such an interest in you and Rocky. Now she's trying to force my hand.'

Phil looked at Gavin over the top of his spectacles.

'Better not state those views to the press, old man, otherwise she can have you up for libel.'

'But it's true, Phil. Don't you see, everything makes sense now? She never really cared two tuppenny damns about me before, and then she suddenly began to ring up and take an interest in me. I thought she was just bored, but now I see what's behind it all. It would suit her very well to be Lady Pelham with a nice fat bank balance. Well, she won't get away with it. I'm going to ring her now.'

Phil guessed his brother-in-law was aching for action of some kind.

'Come, Judith, tea,' he said, getting up and helping her to her feet. 'We'll leave Gavin in peace to make his call.'

Helen was in when the phone rang. She recognized Gavin's voice at once, and said sweetly:

'Darling! What a lovely surprise. I've just this minute got home.'

Gavin's voice was cold and hard.

'Have you by any chance seen the *Western Echo*?'

'Why, no, Gavin. Should I have done so?'

'It's no good playing the innocent with me, Helen. We might as well understand each other right away. The article in the *Echo* leaves me in no doubt at all that somehow or another you've given their reporter a private interview. You've also given him to understand that you and I are engaged.'

Helen was thinking quickly. She'd expected Gavin to be annoyed about the article, but not to be furiously angry. Skilfully she avoided a reply by pretending that the line was bad.

'There's a terrible noise here — I can hardly hear you, Gavin. Where did you say you were speaking from?'

'I'm speaking from Rosemary's, my sister's. The *Echo's* just arrived. What I want to know, Helen, is how you got hold of their reporter. Judith says no one came to the surgery yesterday afternoon when you were there.'

Helen frowned. So Judith was at the farm with Gavin. It looked as if the girl was after him, too. Well, she would not give him up easily.

'I just don't understand what you're talking about, darling,' she protested. 'If I've done anything to upset you, I'm terribly sorry. I'll get a copy of the paper and then perhaps I'll understand what all the fuss is about. Will you be back at work next week, Gavin? If so, I might call in and see you and we'll get it all straightened out.'

He didn't wish to see her, but he realized it might be a good thing if she came back and denied the report in the *Echo* herself. If he were to do so it would appear very ungallant.

He replaced the receiver, uncertain

now as to whether Helen had really been responsible. She'd sounded genuinely surprised and confused.

He felt a deep unease. There was Judith's father to worry about and, more important, Judith herself. He didn't want her to imagine that he was the kind of man to break his promise to one girl and turn his thoughts the next moment to another. She must be able to believe in him and trust him and rely on him, and this was hardly a good beginning.

With a deep sigh, he screwed up the offending article and threw it with a symbolic gesture of disgust into the fire.

14

Olive Bryant sat on the bed watching her daughter pack, her thin pale face anxious and fretful.

'I do hope you are acting for the best, Judith. Your father seemed to think it's a good idea for you to go away — or at least, he was quite happy about it until he read that article in the *Echo*. I don't understand, Judith. *Is* Gavin Pelham really engaged to that model girl?'

Judith sighed. She had arrived home with Gavin this Monday morning in order to pack sufficient of her clothes to last her at least the first few months at Cherry Tree Farm. She had made up her mind on Sunday night that she would accept Rosemary's wonderful offer of a job with sufficient pocket money in return for helping her with the children. She needed time more than anything else in the world in which to straighten out her life.

She'd been home for an hour during which time her mother had never stopped questioning her. It wouldn't have been so bad if she had been able to answer any of the questions. She listened as the wavering voice continued:

'Aren't you still in love with Rocky? He's been on the telephone three times since Friday — I'm sure he's still in love with you, dear. Surely if it's true — about the baby I mean — you ought to marry Rocky. It all seems so terrible, Judith. I just don't understand.'

'Nor do I, Mother,' Judith said as gently as she could. She folded her candlewick dressing-gown and packed it automatically. Strangely, she had been able to put the thought of Rocky's child far back in her mind over the week-end. But Rocky she could not put out of her thoughts so easily.

'I told you Rocky would be home for the day. He's coming round at eleven o'clock, Judith. He said he *must* see you and the poor boy sounded so desperate. I hadn't the heart to say no, though what your father would say if he knew, I dare not imagine.'

Judith looked up sharply.

'*Rocky, coming here?*'

Her first instinct was fear — to avoid seeing him — to hide — go out — not have to talk to him. But then she realized that it would be better to face Rocky and hear what he had to say. Seeing him again might help her to discover if she were still in love with him. She had to know for Gavin's sake.

Gavin! Her heart filled with a sudden warm tenderness. He'd been so incredibly comforting and gentle and understanding. He seemed always to transfer her burdens to his own shoulders and make her feel that none of her worries were important, after all. Was this feeling of irresponsibility he gave her a good thing? Was she taking unwitting advantage of his kindness, counting on his love for her to get her out of her difficulties in the easiest way? She would hate herself if she ever made use of him. Wasn't it true that if he hadn't wanted to marry her, she might now be praying desperately for Rocky to want her still?

Judith continued with her sorting and packing, a fresh wave of uncertainty and apprehension spreading over her, destroying the calm mood of the week-end.

'There's the front door bell now,' Olive Bryant said, jumping to her feet and looking anxiously at Judith. 'It must be Rocky. You'd better show him into the drawing-room, Judith . . . ' She paused, forgetting her own fears and worries and wanting only that her child should be happy.

Judith suddenly longed to call her back. She felt if not exactly close to her mother, a great burning sense of closeness. If only her mother were the kind of woman who could tell her firmly what to do! But she belonged to another generation — to a society who could find only horror and shame in her daughter's predicament, who would condemn the one moment of weakness without taking into account the reason for it.

Judith sighed. How could she expect a woman like her mother to understand? Since she had never been able to discuss even the simple facts of life, what hope had Judith of making her see that this was no dreadful upsurge of sex which had brought her to the point of giving way. It wasn't for herself she had let Rocky make love to her — but for him . . .

Judith walked to the door. At least she and Rocky could talk the same language. Whatever had to be said, they would know what the other meant. If there was no longer love — at least there could be honesty.

With her head held proudly erect, Judith went slowly down the stairs. She opened the front door and her eyes met Rocky's, briefly. Judith's mother followed them into the Victorian drawing-room, asking if there was anything Rocky would like — tea or coffee?

Rocky refused politely and then at last, they were alone. He'd meant to go straight to Judith and take her in his arms. He just didn't care what his father said about his job — his future. Beg her forgiveness, tell her how much he still loved her. But something in the pale, remote face halted him at the first step.

'Sit down, Rocky,' Judith said quietly. As he did so, she seated herself opposite him and looked straight at him from shadowed blue eyes.

'You wanted to see me?'

'It's not true, is it? That you're going to marry Pelham?'

The question burst from him so unexpectedly that Judith's first reaction was of surprise; then her face flushed a deep pink. She realized that he was jealous and in a moment of pure femininity, she was glad!

'Gavin *has* asked me to marry him!' she said gently, although her heart was beating furiously.

'You can't, Judith. *You're my girl*.

You're going to marry me.'

For one short minute she weakened towards him. His girl!

He always called her that. And she had loved him so much . . . She looked at the dark, tousled brown head, the wide, dark-brown eyes and rather full sensuous mouth as if she were seeing him for the first time. He was attractive — young, vibrant, alive — everything that had been lacking in her dull, repressed young life. With his gaiety and energy and enthusiasm and his strong-willed desires, he had brought a great wave of excitement into her life and swept her away on its consequent whirlwind. She had discovered what it was to be kissed — to be attractive to a man — to thrill to his touch and his voice and his maleness. No wonder she had fallen in love! Perhaps she would never be able to put him right out of her heart — Rocky, her first love.

As if sensing her mood, he jumped up and pulled her to her feet so that their bodies were pressed together. The desire for Judith that had been so mysteriously absent, returned now to Rocky more urgent and desperate than before. He wanted her — at any price. If she insisted on marriage, he would agree. Nothing mattered now but that he should have her. It seemed impossible that he had ever contemplated life without her.

But for Judith, it was different. Her body, at first responsive from habit, was suddenly immune to his touch. She twisted her face away from his kiss and as his hands tightened, she began to fight seriously to free herself.

At first, he believed she was afraid lest her mother should come back into the room.

'Don't be silly, Judy!' he whispered hoarsely. 'She meant us to be alone, Judy . . . darling . . . '

But she still struggled against him, suddenly terrified of the strength of his arms and his desire.

'Please, Rocky, *please . . . I don't love you any more . . .* '

He released her abruptly, frustrated and angry, his face sullen.

'You're saying that to hurt me. You're trying to get your own back on me because of what I said last week . . . '

Judith looked at him steadily. Fear was replaced by surprise and pity. He seemed all of a sudden so young — so incredibly immature. Grown-up people didn't try to 'get their own back'.

As if a veil had been drawn from her eyes, she saw him in that instant exactly as he was, an attractive angry boy who was unable to have what he wanted.

'Rocky, please try to understand. It isn't because of anything you've said — it isn't even because of Gavin. It's just that I've suddenly grown up. I don't feel the same about you any more. I'm dreadfully sorry.'

Rocky fastened on Gavin's name with sudden fury. It must be that man who had changed her. Judith might deny it but he knew better.

'He's old!' he flung at her, wanting to hurt her. 'Do you think you'd be happy married to an OLD MAN? It's disgusting — that's what it is — like those stories you read in the paper. I suppose you're after his money — and don't deny it, Judith — I've read how he's come into money — and a title. Lady Pelham — that's who you want to be. You're no better than a cheap little go-getter — '

Two bright spots burning in her white cheeks, Judith walked quickly over to him and slapped his face. He broke off, staring at her, his hands clenching at his sides.

'No woman who does that to me gets away with it. This is the last time you'll see me, Judith. I'm going — and this time, I shan't come back.'

He hurled himself dramatically to the door and paused to see if she would try to detain him. When she didn't move, he was forced to open the door. He didn't want to go — it couldn't end like this — yet pride forbade him apologizing. It was Judith who must apologize. She always had in the past — she would

— she *must* . . .

But she remained like a statue, lifeless, without movement or speech.

'So this really packs it all up!' Rocky was all but shouting the words. 'And to think I nearly chucked up my job — for *you* . . . My father was right — you're not worth it, Judith, and you never were.'

He opened the door and looked at her for the last time. If she would only say something — make some gesture — anything to show that she was sorry . . . but she stood silently watching him, looking at him as if she had never seen him before.

'Oh, to hell with you!' he said, unbearably angry and hurt. And turning away from her, he flung himself out of the room. A moment later, Judith heard the front door slam behind him and knew that it was all over.

She knelt down on the soft blue carpet beneath her feet and rested her head against the arm of the chair. The scene had completely exhausted her and she felt sick. Rocky's words were ringing round her mind like electric shocks.

'*Go-getter — after his money — to hell with you . . . wasted my time . . . .*' He'd made their love for one another sound so cheap, so rotten, so shabby. Had it been like that? No, no, *no*! Was this how everyone felt when love was gone — hating and hurting and somehow belittled and ashamed?

'Judith! Whatever are you doing there? Where's Rocky? He hasn't *gone*?'

Wearily, Judith stood up and faced her mother's ever-anxious gaze.

'Yes, Mother, he's gone. I don't think we'll see each other any more. It's over for good this time.'

Mrs. Bryant didn't know what to do. The look of pain so apparent on Judith's face worried her. Was the girl in love with that young man still, in spite of everything? Had she and Harold been wrong to part them? Harold had been so sure — and yet — and yet she couldn't bear the look on Judith's face — like a trapped deer.

Helplessly, she patted her daughter's arm.

'Try not to mind too much, dear! *Tout casse, tout passe*, you know. Besides, dear, he really wasn't quite suitable, now was he? If only it weren't for — for the baby . . . ' she shuddered in spite of her wish to help her daughter.

'Don't worry, Mother!' Judith said, unable to bear this well-meant sympathy. 'I expect you're quite right and it'll all turn out for the best.'

She was too tired and too miserable to explain that she was regretting not the loss of Rocky but the disillusion of love itself.

'Father's sure to ask me what has happened . . . ' Olive Bryant tried not to burden Judith with further questions but a lifetime of obedience to Harold was stronger than her pity for her child. 'Am I to say it's finished? I suppose you can't stay till he gets home, Judith?'

Judith put an arm round her mother's shoulders and gave her a brief hug.

'I'm afraid I can't, Mummy!' The childish name slipped out. 'Gavin has promised to drive me down to the farm after he has finished work.'

She saw the resignation in the lined face and was overcome by a sudden urgent need for understanding.

'Mother, why did you marry Father? Did you love him? Do you still love him?'

Mrs. Bryant looked flustered and unhappy.

'But of course I do, dear! He's my husband.'

'But that's no reason!' Judith burst out. 'Were you ever *in love* with him, Mother?'

'I don't know what you mean, Judith. Of course I loved him. At first, we were a little strange to one another — we hadn't ever been alone before our honeymoon — my parents always chaperoned me, you know. But Harold — your father — was very kind and forbearing . . . ' She paused, remembering the shock of a honeymoon long since buried in a forgotten part of her mind. 'He worked hard for me and has taken care of me and been good to me. Of course I love him, just as he loves me.'

Judith let her arms drop to her sides. There seemed no 'of course' about it. Surely kindness and forbearance and care of one human being by another wasn't all of love? There must be more to love than gratitude and familiarity.

'I'll ask Gavin,' she thought and then in the blinding flash of truth, she knew. With Gavin there was everything. He was gentle and sweet and kind and understanding, and when he had held her and kissed her — there had been passion and desire, too.

'Oh, Gavin, Gavin,' she thought, her whole body trembling. 'I love you — I love you and I didn't know. You are what I want — what I need — what I desire — *you* . . .'

When Gavin had first told her he loved her and wanted to marry her, her mind and heart had been full of Rocky and the future had had little meaning for her. In some peculiar way, Gavin had managed at the week-end to make her forget about the baby and to surround her with his love and care, with complete disregard for himself. She had been selfishly concerned only with her own life and its problems; had never considered what a tremendous act of unselfishness Gavin's offer to marry her had been.

She knew she could never go through with it now. No matter how much Gavin might argue that he loved her, and that they could be happy together, she could not go to him with Rocky's child. If she truly loved him, she would go out of his life. She must go right away, where Gavin wouldn't find her, and let him forget about her. She had no right to love him. He deserved someone much better than herself. She wished with desperate ache that she'd never known Rocky, never allowed him to make love to her. Now it was all too late.

But *was* it too late? Gavin knew she

might be having a baby — had asked her to marry him in spite of it. No, she could never take advantage of his chivalry — or his love. To think of doing so was to belittle the purity and depth of her newfound love for him. What might have seemed possible before was out of the question now.

But would Gavin let her go without a fight? It did not seem probable if he ever guessed she loved him.

'I'll have to lie to him,' she thought wearily. 'Pretend I still love Rocky — somehow convince him he means nothing to me. I can't stay on at the Hughes now. After the week-end, I'll go away.'

She couldn't bring herself to talk to her mother. When she had made up her mind to go, what to do, she would write.

Somehow she managed to get through the day, and when Gavin called for her soon after five o'clock she was waiting for him in the hall with two suitcases. The warmth in his voice and eyes as he

313

greeted her cheerfully were almost too much for her. Blinded by tears, she kissed her mother quickly and followed Gavin out to the car.

For a while, he talked cheerfully about the day's work. He seemed not to notice her silence until they were well clear of the town, and then he said, suddenly:

'You're terribly quiet, Judith. You're feeling all right? You haven't had a scene with your father? If something's upset you, I want to know what it is.'

Glad of the darkness of the interior of the car, Judith said:

'I saw Rocky, Gavin. Mother had told him on the phone last night that I would be home today and he called round this morning.'

Gavin's heart missed a beat. He'd known that sooner or later Judith would meet the boy again, but he'd not expected it so soon and he was afraid of what had transpired.

'Well?' he prompted, gently.

In a small, toneless voice she told

him Rocky wanted to marry her; that she still loved him. Gavin did not interrupt her, but she felt the tenseness of his body beside her and saw his knuckles whiten as he clenched the steering-wheel.

'Oh, darling, darling!' she thought. 'If only you knew how much I love *you*. Everything I'm saying to you is a lie.'

Despite her effort to stay completely remote from him, she said brokenly:

'I'm so sorry, Gavin. You can't begin to know how terrible I feel.'

With an enormous effort, Gavin stilled the great aching blow of disappointment her words had dealt him. He never doubted that she spoke the truth. Rosemary had warned him that her quarrel with Rocky probably meant little more than a lovers' tiff and that Judith might find herself still in love with him when they met again. But because he'd wanted it otherwise, he'd refused to let the thought worry him. During the weekend when he'd held her in his arms and kissed her, and she'd seemed so contented and happy, he'd begun seriously to hope that she might be falling in love with *him*.

Fool that he was to imagine that Judith might see him as an equal. Because he felt so young, young in the first delight of loving her, he'd tricked himself into imagining there was hope.

'You mustn't be sorry, Judith,' he said with a great effort. 'I'm happy for you that it's all working out right in the end.'

They sat in a wretched, unbearable silence, each lost in their own private misery. Judith tried not to think of the months of loneliness that lay ahead. She wondered if she would ever find the courage to face the future alone. She knew she would have to cut herself off completely from her parents, as well as from Gavin and the Hughes. And Gavin — would he turn to Helen? And if he did, would he be happy with her?

The long drive was this time torture for both of them. When they drove up to Cherry Tree Farm, each felt a tremendous sense of relief that in a few minutes they would no longer be alone.

Although it was not yet seven o'clock, Judith excused herself at once saying that she didn't feel like supper and wanted only to go to bed. Gavin thought bitterly that it was his company now that embarrassed her, and that she was trying to avoid him. He couldn't know that she was really afraid, not of him, but of Rosemary's thoughtful gaze and of betraying her true feelings. Artifice was so foreign to her that she was already feeling the strain of the last hour and wasn't sure for how long she could keep this up.

With a longing to confide in someone, Gavin cornered Rosemary in the big kitchen and told her bluntly that it was 'all off'.

Rosemary looked at her brother with dismay.

'Oh, I am so sorry, Gavin. Phil and I had begun to hope that . . . well the fact is, we both like Judith and although at first I was afraid you'd be making a mistake, I'd completely come round to your point of view. I think she could make you happy.'

'And I could have made her happy, I'm sure of it!' Gavin burst out despairingly. 'What's more, I'm sure that boy can't. He's only a kid, Rosemary, and Judith needs looking after. I'm not saying this just because I want her for myself, I'm more than ever convinced that he's no good to her.'

'Even so, Gavin, you can't choose a husband for someone else. They have to make up their minds for themselves. And Judith must love him, to have been able to forgive him so much. You'll just have to face up to it, Gavin, and so shall I. You know, I'm almost as sorry as you are. Phil, too; we all like her.'

With a now familiar feeling of helplessness, Gavin sat down wearily, his elbows on the table, his chin resting in his hands.

'Perhaps I'd find it easier to accept my *congé* if Judith seemed happier. But she sat in the car barely saying a word and looking . . . well, I can only describe it as miserable.'

'You're quite sure you've got the facts right?' Rosemary asked, sympathetically. 'You think it's definite this time?'

Gavin nodded. He raised a tortured face.

'Life can be cruel, can't it? It's taken me thirty years to fall in love and find the girl I'd like to marry, and then she has to be in love with another man.'

Rosemary offered him the only comfort there was.

'I'll have a long talk with Judith tomorrow, and if there's any hope, Gavin, I'll let you know at once. But I can't try to influence her in any way and I'm sure you wouldn't want me to. Neither of us can know what that boy's really made of. And even if he is weak, marriage to Judith and the responsibility of a child may pull him together.'

She went upstairs before she prepared the supper, to look in on Judith, but the girl was already in bed, her face turned away from the door. Rosemary wasn't convinced that Judith was sleeping, but neither was it in her nature to force herself where she wasn't wanted. She went downstairs to join the two men, her heart strangely uneasy. She couldn't see how anyone was going to derive much happiness from this new state of affairs, least of all Gavin whom she adored and wanted so much to be happy. She hoped desperately that if Judith were lost to him, he wouldn't turn back on the rebound to Helen Rowe. Although she'd never met her, there was something about that hard, beautiful face which she mistrusted. But when she questioned Gavin as to what he had done about the newspaper article, he shrugged his shoulders and said with complete lack of interest:

'I'd really rather have nothing more to do with Helen. Frankly, I couldn't care less why she gave that story to the reporter — if she did. I've certainly no wish to see her to discuss it.'

Rosemary sighed.

'It all seems very odd. One can't help feeling a little superstititious, Gavin.

Things seem to have gone badly for us all since you heard you were heir to Uncle Basil's estate.'

Gavin was at last able to smile.

'If I thought it could change things, I'd willingly give up the title and the money.'

He left soon after supper looking heavy-hearted and tired. If she hadn't liked Judith so much, Rosemary would have hated her at this moment for bringing Gavin so much unhappiness. But as she told Phil, as they sat in comfortable quietness by the fire, one simply could not in all fairness blame Judith for the way things had turned out. She'd never tried to attract Gavin, and the running had been all his making.

One had only to know her for a little while to realize that for all that happened in her young life, she had remained inherently an innocent child.

'I wish there were something we could do,' she reiterated. Rosemary little knew that tomorrow would bring the chance she so desired.

15

It was barely nine o'clock when Gavin reached home, tired, cold, and utterly dispirited. So lost in thought was he that it wasn't until he was putting the car in the little brick garage that he realized there was a light burning in the downstairs room. Surely, he thought, Mrs. Dawson can't still be here. Was something wrong?

He walked towards the house apprehensively and turned his key in the lock. Standing on the threshold, he knew at once who his visitor was. He could recognize that peculiar, heady perfume that only Helen used.

His first reaction was to walk quickly out again. He wasn't even curious as to how she had got in, or why she was here. She meant nothing to him now, and he simply didn't wish to be bothered with her.

But while he stood hesitantly, wondering if he could slip away unnoticed, the sitting-room door opened and Helen stood there, calm, poised, with a friendly welcome on her face.

'Darling, how lovely to see you, and so early, too. Mrs. Dawson didn't seem to think that you would be back before midnight.'

'I'm flattered that you should have thought it worth while waiting so long for me,' Gavin said sarcastically.

He walked past her into the sitting-room, and seeing she had found his drink cupboard, helped himself from the bottle of whisky and sat down by the gas-fire without removing his coat.

Helen stood in the doorway, watching him. She knew that this might be a crucial moment in their association and that she must be tactful at all costs. She closed the door behind her, and walking gracefully over to his chair, rested a hand lightly on his shoulder.

'Darling, I know you're frightfully cross with me about that article, but at least you'll hear my side of it since I've come all this way to explain to you?'

Gavin's good manners were so instinctive that whatever his feelings towards her, he could not lounge in his chair while she remained standing. He got up and poured her a drink, and did not sit down until she was seated opposite him. Not without humour, he noted the expensive, fashionable white coat and thought how incongruous it looked against the stiff horse-hair sofa with its cheap moquette cover.

Helen mistook the smile for a weakening towards her. She leant closer to him and said with a well-simulated ring of conviction in her tone:

'You do realize, Gavin, that I wasn't to blame? I give you my word I didn't tell that reporter we were engaged. I merely told him we were old friends and when he asked me point-blank if we were going to get married, I told him it wasn't for me to answer the question. I see now that my reply may have misled him. But, naturally, I wasn't to realize this at the time. I'm terribly sorry, darling.'

'I can't see why you couldn't tell him outright there was no question of an engagement.'

Helen leant back against the uncomfortable sofa, looking at Gavin provocatively through long, blackened lashes.

'I suppose I've been rather a fool. But because of what had been between us, and because I love you, I was fool enough to hope that one day we might . . . ' she broke off, with well-feigned modesty.

Gavin gave her a quick, searching look. Had he in fact misjudged her? Instinct told him 'no', and yet there was something soft and shy about her which he'd never seen in her before. Was she really fond of him?

'You still haven't explained how you came to be talking to a reporter at all,' he said thoughtfully.

Helen sat back, completely sure of herself.

'That's one of the things I wanted to tell you, Gavin. You didn't know it, but my car broke down on Friday on my way back to Town and I was forced to get a hired car into Yeovil. Normally, it would have been a ghastly nuisance but I didn't mind too much because I was sure I should see you. I kept ringing your surgery, and the house, but it seemed you'd gone to your sister's. Saturday morning I called at the surgery and missed you again, and that's when I ran into this reporter. He'd been trying to get hold of you, too. I didn't really give him an interview. We were just chatting to pass the time while we waited for you. So you see, darling, you very unkindly jumped to the worst possible conclusion.'

Gavin looked slightly discomfited. The way Helen described what had happened made it all sound innocent enough.

'Oh, well!' He gave a deep sigh. 'I don't suppose any of it matters much. Incidentally, Helen, I asked my brother-in-law, who happens to be a solicitor, to get the *Echo* to deny the bit about our engagement. They'll no doubt print an apology in due course.'

He could not fail to notice the sudden swift rush of angry colour to Helen's cheeks, but he mistook anger for embarrassment. He didn't want to hurt her, but at the same time it was best if she understood that he had no intention of marrying anybody, now that he couldn't have Judith.

Quite bluntly, he told her that there could never be anyone but Judith in his life.

Thinking it over later, he had to admit that she took it extremely well. She said how sorry she was and how much she wished she could do something to help and repeated over and over again how upset she was to think that the article in the *Echo* might have been partially responsible for Judith's change of heart. Gavin told her that nothing she had said or done could have affected the position, since Judith had never really stopped loving Rockingham.

Oddly enough, he'd found it a great comfort to be able to talk to her hour after hour about his love for Judith. Helen proved a wonderfully sympathetic listener and seemed completely to understand why he should feel as he did about Judith.

She'd tried to knock some commonsense into him, too, to make him see that Judith might be happier in the end with someone younger, and more especially since Rocky was the father of her child. Before she left at midnight, she had very nearly convinced him that there was far more to Rocky than he'd been able to see; that because he loved Judith himself, he'd been unable to appreciate the boy's qualities and had been blinded to them by jealousy.

Lying alone in the cold, hard bed, seeking the sleep that wouldn't come, he realized that his relationship with Helen had taken a completely new guise. She no longer had the power to attract him, since his mind and heart were filled with Judith, but he was glad of her friendship and her understanding and her sympathy. He'd arranged to lunch with her tomorrow, and at least this was something to look forward to in a day that would otherwise be completely wretched. At least it would afford him the chance to talk of Judith and this was a tiny comfort to his aching heart.

Helen returned to her hotel highly satisfied with her evening's work. In his wretched frame of mind, Gavin had been far more susceptible than she had dared hope. Boring as it might be for her to listen to his constant mention of Judith, she could see that this was the right line to take. It would only be a matter of time before he started to need her as the last link with the girl, and so gradually she, Helen, would become indispensable to him.

* * *

Gavin sat in the surgery reading with a fresh wave of incredulous amazement the letter that had arrived that afternoon from his uncle's solicitor. It seemed he was to come into the princely sum of eighty thousand pounds. His mind tried to grapple with the size of the fortune that he might reasonably expect when the coffee plantation in Kenya was sold.

He read the letter for the third time, trying to feel as he imagined other men must feel when they had it in black-and-white that they were really rich. Eighty thousand pounds. Enough to buy twenty thousand practices, he thought with sudden humour. At any rate, he'd be able to pay off the mortgage on his own and buy all the modern equipment he longed for. He might even be able to branch out with his own boarding kennels and employ one or two girls to . . . He broke off his train of thought, abruptly aware that like every other train of thought it only led him back to Judith. How was it possible that he'd once wanted his career for its own sake? It seemed now as if he had only been ambitious because somewhere deep down inside him he'd known that Judith would come along.

Yet he knew it wasn't true. He'd wanted to work with animals because he loved them and because it gave him joy as well as a livelihood to make them well again. Somehow he must try to retrieve this desire to do well for its own sake. Lots of hard work might help him forget, and in this way the money wasn't going to help. There wouldn't be the same necessity for hard work and hours of careful planning how best to spend his meagre income. He'd be able to buy what he wanted now — walk into a shop and say: 'I'll have that, and that, and that . . . ' How different from the day when he had spent a whole evening in his surgery debating whether to spend a few pounds on a steriliser or on some new badly-needed instruments.

He put the letter away in the drawer of his desk, but the words still danced before his eyes. Eighty thousand pounds. With so much money, he could have bought Judith a beautiful house and let her furnish it exactly as she desired. The house could have been large enough to include a surgery so that they'd always be near to one another. They could afford a decent car, holidays, and, not least, a large family. The children could go to good schools and have ponies of their own to ride. And still there'd have been enough over to help Rosemary and Phil and their kids. Well, at least, he could still help them. As soon as the money was in the bank he'd see his solicitor about a Deed of Covenant for his nephew and nieces.

Once again, his train of thought had taken him to Judith. He beat his clenched fist upon the desk in a sudden wave of angry despair. What a fool he'd ever been to hope! How mad to believe that because she'd returned his kiss with soft, gentle lips, that she must be beginning to care.

He thought ironically of his statement to Judith's father. 'I'm going to marry Judith.' At the time, it had seemed as simple as that. He'd believed Rockingham had finished with her and, conceited fool that he was, had taken it for granted that Judith would turn to him. The trouble was he had ceased to think and feel as a man of thirty, since he realized he was in love with her. And what right had he to suppose that she would see him as a boy in love, too? He knew that at seventeen, thirty could seem old.

He stood up and paced the surgery restlessly. Mrs. Dawson would have prepared his supper and left it in the oven for him. He ought to go home. But this gloom, with memories of Judith, held him prisoner. Standing beside her desk, he could still believe that she was here. When he closed his eyes, he could see the smooth, shining head and the gentle curve of her back as she leant over her work. He could almost believe that if the telephone were to ring, he would hear her cool, clear voice saying, as she always did, with that surprisingly businesslike efficiency: 'Mr. Pelham's surgery. Can I help you?'

He sat down suddenly at her desk, and supported his tortured head in his hands.

'*Oh, Judith, Judith!*' he thought, with

a wild, unhappy longing. *'Come back to me. Don't leave me. I can't live without you. Come back to me, Judith. I need you so!'*

The shrill ring of the telephone pierced his mind with startling suddenness. Automatically, he lifted the receiver and said, as Judith always did:

'Mr. Pelham's surgery. Can I help you?'

Rosemary's familiar voice brought him back to reality.

'Oh, Gavin, I've been trying to get you for hours. I never thought you'd be at the surgery and I've been ringing your house. Are you listening, Gavin? I've some incredible news.'

16

The children were playing quietly in the nursery while the rain poured incessantly from a grey sky into the bare, sodden garden.

Inside the kitchen, it was warm and friendly and only the atmosphere was strained as Judith helped Rosemary with the preparations for lunch. This constraint between the two women was something quite new and both felt it acutely. Judith with anxiety lest Rosemary should guess the real reason for her inner despair, and Rosemary puzzled that Judith should not be more radiant and talkative now that her future was at last decided.

At last the awkward silence became too much for Rosemary and she said, bluntly:

'Aren't you feeling well, Judith?'

'Oh, yes, I feel fine,' Judith said quickly. 'I had a long night's sleep.'

'Then what *is* wrong?' Rosemary persisted. 'You've great shadows under your eyes and you're so tensed up. You've twice nearly dropped that dish. You're not feeling sick, are you?'

'No, of course not. Whatever made you think . . . ?' She broke off, her face suddenly flushed with embarrassment as she realized the reason for Rosemary's question.

Rosemary took the dish from Judith's hand and pushed her gently into one of the wooden kitchen chairs, then sat down beside her.

'I don't want to probe, Judith, but it seems to me that you need someone to talk to about this baby. For instance, have you seen your doctor?'

Judith traced a line of the scrubbed table-top with her finger-nail.

'Oh, no, Rosemary. I couldn't possibly go to him.'

Rosemary raised her eyebrows.

'But have you seen *a* doctor?'

She saw Judith shake her fair head in negation.

A little shocked and puzzled, Rosemary said:

'Then how d'you know you're having a baby? You must have seen someone?'

Judith shook her head again.

Rosemary said, quietly:

'Then I'd like you to see my doctor, Judith. I think for everyone's sake, and most of all your own, you ought to find out if you really are going to have a baby. Will you let me give him a ring and ask him to come round? He's very nice, and there's no reason he should know that you're unmarried, if you'd rather not.'

Judith looked at Rosemary helplessly. There seemed little point in having her fears confirmed. But if Rosemary thought it necessary, she had no reason to refuse. She herself no longer doubted the outcome of such an examination.

Rosemary, however, although she could give no reason for it, had certainly begun to hope. Phil had often teased her about her 'woman's intu-ition' but after years of marriage, he'd finally accepted that without any logical reason she was frequently right. This same intuition made her ponder anew the question of Judith and Rocky. She could understand that with the threat of an unwanted child hanging over her head, the young couple might not appear as radiantly happy as they would in other circumstances. But Judith's complete apathy seemed to Rosemary to be more than a little odd. She was greatly relieved when Judith agreed to see her doctor and, wasting no time, managed to arrange for him to call that afternoon.

She waited anxiously while the doctor was with Judith. She tried to tell herself that the young girl meant nothing to her; that Judith's future didn't even concern Gavin any more, but nevertheless she had grown so fond of her that it was as if her own daughter were upstairs, or a younger sister perhaps. When Doctor Audley came downstairs, she went to meet him with an eager hopefulness she could not conceal.

'I don't think you have the slightest cause to worry about your friend,' Doctor Audley said, sensing her concern. 'I've questioned her thoroughly and it's my belief that she's over-wrought and run-down. It's surprising, you know, how fear of pregnancy can very often effect a delay. Really, it's quite refreshing to find such innocence in these days. Unless I had heard her with my own ears, I'd never have believed that a teenager of today could know so little about the physical union of a man and woman. She was a little shy with me at first but it wasn't long before she talked quite freely. I can say quite definitely that it would have been impossible for her to have a baby as a result of the incompleteness of the incident. I've no doubt the released tension will restore everything to normal in a few days.'

Rosemary drew a huge sigh of relief. Old Doctor Audley wasn't given to speculations. He would not allow her to pass on this news to Judith if he felt there was the slightest possibility of her being plunged back into renewed fear and anxiety, later.

As soon as the doctor had gone, she ran upstairs to Judith's room and was amazed to find her lying face downwards on the bed, sobbing as if her heart would break.

'Judith, darling!' she said, sitting down and putting an arm round the shaking shoulders. 'You can't cry now. It's going to be all right. Dr. Audley said I could tell you that he's absolutely sure there isn't going to be a baby. It only existed in your imagination. You've nothing to worry about any more.'

For a moment or two longer, Judith continued to cry, and then she sat up suddenly and said:

'I'm not going to marry Rocky. I don't love him. I only told Gavin so because I knew I had no right to his love and I wanted him to forget about me.'

'I felt something was wrong,' Rosemary said triumphantly. 'I knew you weren't happy.'

'I think I stopped loving Rocky when we were at Gretna Green. I hated it up there — it was awful. I think we both felt awful. I know Rocky was terribly disappointed in me. He wanted to make love to me, and because I wouldn't say 'yes' he felt forced to marry me. After we came home, it was worse than ever. I'm sure he didn't mean to, but he gave me the feeling that I'd cheated him out of something. That's why . . . that's why I let him make love to me. I only realized for certain that he really didn't love me when I told him that I thought I was going to have a baby. Even then, I couldn't bring myself to admit that I'd loved, not Rocky as he was, but as I wanted him to be. Then, last week-end, Gavin kissed me. It wasn't just the kiss, although I couldn't understand at the time why I should like it so much, but everything about that day. When I'm with Gavin, I don't have to pretend that I'm someone else. He gives me the feeling of being protected and loved and cared for. He makes me feel like a woman, complete in some way I can't explain. When I saw Rocky again he seemed such a boy, not really a man at all, and it was as if I'd grown up suddenly and left him behind. Can you understand what I'm trying to say, Rosemary?'

Rosemary smiled.

'I think what you're really trying to say is that you're in love with Gavin,' she said gently. 'When Gavin first brought you down here, I was afraid he was going to catch you on the rebound. But it hasn't worked out that way, has it? He's caught you at the point of growing up, and I think it's wonderful, Judith. Don't you see that there's nothing now to stand between you any more?'

Judith shook her head.

'But I can't possibly marry him, Rosemary. Even if I'm not having a baby after all, there'd always be the memory of Rocky between us. It wouldn't be fair to Gavin. I love him too much to offer him second-best.'

Rosemary took Judith's hands in hers and held them tightly.

'That's madness, Judith. Rocky needn't stand between you unless *you* let him. After all, Gavin knew about your association with him before he fell in love with you. He told me he wanted to marry you, so he must in his own mind be more than prepared to forgive and forget. Besides, you don't imagine that Gavin's led a completely blameless past, do you? It isn't what's gone before that matters, Judith. It's the future. That might have been more difficult for you both if there'd been Rocky's child as a constant reminder, but now you can both forget about it.'

The colour came back into Judith's cheeks, as Rosemary's kindly advice brought the first ray of hope.

'I wish I were older,' Judith sighed. 'I wish I were the same age as Gavin.'

Rosemary smiled.

'That's the last thing in the world you should want, Judith. And you should remember that Gavin loves you because you're as you are. If you were sophisticated and experienced, and a woman of the world, he mightn't love you at all. Women like Helen, for instance, may attract a man, but despite everything you read about the emancipation of women, it's the girls like you men want to marry. Now tidy your hair, Judith, and since it's stopped raining we'll take the children for a walk. I'm going to ring Gavin. Unless I'm much mistaken, he'll be down here as quick as the old brake will bring him.'

Rosemary glanced at the clock on the mantelpiece. It was nearly ten. Gavin should be here by now. Unless, of course, his battered old shooting-brake had finally given way under the strain of so many journeys to and from the farm.

Rosemary was affected by Judith's nervousness. She understood quite well how the younger girl was feeling. Now that everything had been resolved, Judith had been unable to rid herself of the feeling of inferiority and uncertainty that had clouded her life for the last few months.

Judith longed for, and at the same time dreaded, the moment when Gavin would arrive.

She knew she wasn't beautiful, that she was unsophisticated, and shy. She had none of Helen's glamour and poise — nothing at all to offer him. With his looks, his new title, and the money which would soon be his, he would be able to choose a wife from a hundred other much more interesting and attractive girls. It seemed incredible that he should love *her*.

'Do stop worrying, Judith,' Rosemary broke in on her train of thought. 'You'll see, everything will be all right when he comes.'

Nevertheless, when Judith heard the sound of the car wheels on the gravel drive, her heart jolted painfully and the palms of her hands became suddenly wet with nervousness. Rosemary stood up and nodded to Phil.

'Come with me and let him in,' she said pointedly.

'But the door's not locked — ' he

345

broke off, realizing from Rosemary's expression that he was expected to be tactful and leave Judith alone.

But Judith, suddenly terrified, clung to his arm.

'You wait here with me, Phil,' she begged.

He gently pulled away from her and gave her a kindly smile.

'Gavin won't eat you, my dear,' he said, and obediently followed his wife out of the room.

Judith stood alone and vulnerable in the middle of the room. She heard the sound of Gavin's voice in the hall, and then Phil's, urging him to come in out of the cold. Rosemary said she was going to make some coffee and told Gavin to go into the sitting-room where he'd find Judith.

Then the door opened and Gavin came in.

He closed it quietly behind him and stood there for one long moment, staring at her.

During the long, cold drive down,

he'd thought of nothing else but this moment. He'd been afraid that Rosemary and Phil would still be around, and that it might be hours before he was alone with Judith. He might have known that Rosemary would have organized things more tactfully. What a wonderful sister she'd proved to be!

All Judith's fears were suddenly gone. The sight of Gavin in that old tweed greatcoat which she'd hung up so often behind the surgery door was wonderfully familiar. She could almost believe that he would throw his coat over the nearest chair and say to her: 'Beastly cold night, Judith. Any urgent calls?'

Without thinking, she moved forward, reaching out her arms to take his coat, just as she had done a hundred times before. But this time, it was different. For Gavin caught hold of her outstretched hands, and gently pulling her close to him, laid his cheek against her hair.

'Oh, Judith, my darling, my dearest love. You don't know how I've longed for this moment . . . '

He put his hand beneath her chin and tilted her face so that he could look into those beautiful, sad eyes that had so often haunted his dreams. But this time, he could see only joy and happiness shining from their depths.

Shyly, she reached up a small white hand and gently traced the outline of his mouth. It was the first small gesture of love she had ever made towards him, and his heart began to beat furiously. With a carefully controlled passion, he kissed her softly on the mouth. She was incredibly young and had suffered so much, he couldn't bear the thought of frightening her or hurting her by letting her know of the turbulent emotions her nearness evoked.

But now he was to discover a new Judith. A strangely exciting and passionate woman beneath the childlike exterior. She wound her arms round his neck and kissed him without reservation. As his arms tightened round her, she clung to him more fiercely and he felt her body tremble beneath his touch.

He drew away from her reluctantly, and removing his overcoat he flung it aside. Then with a quick, easy grace he gathered her into his arms and carried her across to the sofa by the fire. She lay against him, quiet now, and smiling at him with a look of such tenderness and love that he could not trust himself to speak to her. He kissed her eyes, her soft white throat, and her two small hands, and then once again, her lips. Then she laid a finger across his mouth as if to quieten him, and said:

'I love you so very much, Gavin. I never realized it was possible to feel like this.'

His heart sang in a great rush of joy and thankfulness.

He knew that this was no love on the rebound. Her last words gave him all the proof he'd wanted that she'd never really loved Rockingham. Just as he had never loved Evelyn or Helen. It was the first true love for them both, and he never doubted that it would last.

Judith was suddenly shy again. She

tried to sit up and straighten her hair, saying anxiously:

'We can't just lie here, Gavin. Supposing Rosemary comes in with the coffee?'

He gave her a quick, contented laugh and drew her back into his arms.

'So what?' he teased. 'We are an engaged couple now.'

Then his face was suddenly serious.

'You haven't said that you *will* marry me, Judith. You will, won't you?'

Judith's reply was equally serious.

'If you're absolutely sure, Gavin, that you want me.'

Gavin's hands were gripping her arms, unaware that he was hurting her.

'Want you!' he echoed. 'My God, Judith, you can't begin to know what it's been like since I realized I was in love with you. I've been unable to think of anything but you, day and night. Even when I'm working, your image has come into my mind, tormenting me, haunting me. I don't know how I could have found a way to go on living without you. When you told me you were going to marry

Rockingham — and I believed you — I tried to force you out of my thoughts, but you stayed with me all the time. Your little ghost hung about the surgery to trap me when I paused for a moment in what I was doing. You were beside me in the car when I did my rounds. I would see you in the street and then when I approached you it would turn out to be some other fair girl, and I'd be forced to realize that you were miles away and that I might never see you any more. I never understood before why poets wrote of love as a torment. Now I understand.'

She was so deeply moved that she could find no words for him, but she longed to erase the suffering she'd inadvertently caused him. At last, she cried:

'I'll never leave you again, darling. If you've got to go back to the surgery tomorrow, I shall come with you. Wherever you go, I want to be with you.'

There was time for only one long kiss which symbolized for each of them their real betrothal. Later, there would be an announcement in the papers, an engagement ring, and as soon as possible a wedding. But it was at this single moment in time that each gave their heart unreservedly into the other's care.

Then Rosemary banged on the door and came clattering in with a laden coffee tray, Phil following with a dusty bottle in his hand.

'Rosemary insists that Judith will want coffee, but I have a feeling that the occasion demands champagne.'

Gavin held Judith's hand tightly in his own, and they were relaxed and smiling as they looked up at the couple who had been so good to them.

'If that's one of the bottles you put down for Terry's twenty-first,' Gavin told Phil, 'then I'd hate to rob my nephew. Coffee will do just as well to celebrate.'

But Phil was already pulling the cork and Rosemary said, laughing:

'Good heavens, Gavin, with all your money you can put down a whole cellar for Terry. At least let us enjoy one bottle now.'

Gavin looked surprised.

'I keep forgetting I'm rich!'

He looked down at Judith adoringly.

'Do you realize, darling, that you're marrying money? I shall be able to give you anything in the world you want. What do you want, Judith? I shall go out and buy it tomorrow. There must be something you've always wanted to have and couldn't afford to buy.'

Oblivious to Rosemary's and Phil's company, Judith looked into Gavin's grey eyes and said softly:

'I don't want anything but you.'

Phil gave a pleased shout, and tossed the champagne cork into the air.

'Don't you believe a word of it, Gavin,' he teased his brother-in-law. 'Just wait until you've been married a few years and you'll find she'll be asking for a new cooker and a fur coat, and a couple of kids, and a new house and — '

'If you don't shut up, Phil, I shall throw something at you,' Rosemary interrupted.

Then unexpectedly, she linked her

arm in her husband's and planted a swift kiss on his cheek.

'If you two manage to be as happy as we are, I'll be quite content for you both,' she said shakily.

And as Phil bent his head to kiss her, Gavin drew Judith back into his arms.

THE END